The Innovative Secrets of

Steve Jobs

The Innovative Secrets of

Steve Jobs

PRADEEP THAKUR

PRABHAT
PRAKASHAN

Published by
PRABHAT PRAKASHAN PVT. LTD.
4/19 Asaf Ali Road,
New Delhi-110002 (INDIA)
e-mail: prabhatbooks@gmail.com

ISBN 978-93-5521-835-3

THE INNOVATIVE SECRETS OF STEVE JOBS
by Pradeep Thakur

Edition
First, 2023

Price
₹ 300 (Rupees Three Hundred Only)

Printed at
Japan Art, Delhi

Editor's Note

Founder of Apple and Pixar, Steve Jobs was a pioneer of technology, who invented the Macintosh personal computer for common people. He then went on to invent the revolutionary iPod, a music player, which transformed the world of music industry forever as the iPod paved the way for the development of the iPhone. Jobs combined the strengths of mobile phone and computer in iPhone and thus brought the entire strengths of information technology to the palm of man's hand.

Before making a comeback to Apple, Steve Jobs had entered the field computer animation along with Pixar Animation Studio and made high-quality animated feature films like Toy Story, which prompted the Industry giant The Walt Disney Company to take over Pixar valuing it at 7.4 billion dollars.

The last innovation of Jobs' life was the Tablet Computer iPad through which he had largely done away with the requirement of a personal computer. In fact, in the form of iPad, Jobs wanted to create equipment, which could extend mind's processing power on its small screen along with all types of information of the world.

It is also an interesting fact that in the entire technology industry Steve Jobs was a revolutionary innovator who was never afraid of killing his products. With the advent of Internet-based E-commerce, Jobs inventions proved to be revolutionary, and they had to be incorporated in Apple's commerce ecosystem-iTune store. Customers started clamouring for Apple products and company's financial outcomes asserted its leadership in common markets, and under the charismatic leadership and watchful eye of Steve Jobs, Apple began to be counted among the most successful companies in the history of technology companies.

Jobs had won the heart and mind of the entire planet's users through his products by making them attractive and easy to use, despite their technical complexities. Apple's every product was not only unusual with a superior touch but elegant too. To maintain Apple's lead, Jobs kept pushing suppliers to measure up to new standards on the one hand, and leading a small team of talented engineers kept challenging them for development of new apps.

The influence of Indian spirituality had groomed Steve Jobs as a visionary leader different from his western friends. This was the reason, why he proved to be capable and successful in focusing on needs and challenges of future rather than present. Spiritual intensity had made Jobs capable of imagining new things for 'Think Different', which others could not digest. This was the reason why technology reviewers would go overboard in praising Jobs, whenever he inaugurated any new product; it was followed by long queues of customers waiting outside Apple Stores in the night to get it first early next morning.

Also, all this was the magic of Steve Jobs' management formula which I have attempted to capture in this book.

I believe that this book will help all you informed readers learn the great management art of Steve Jobs.

❑

Contents

❑

Brief Biography of Steve Jobs

No compilation of the foremost digital entrepreneurs of this age can be complete without a bit on Steve Jobs. Inventor, innovator and businessman—Steve Jobs revolutionized the way people communicate and access information. According to US registry records, he filed no less than 346 patents but he is especially remembered as the brains behind game-changing inventions like the Apple personal computer, Macbook, iPod, iPad and of course the iPhone which not only forced the mobile phone industry to shake off its lethargy and innovate but in fact changed human trends in communication, recreation, commerce and information.

Brief Biography

Born as Steven Paul Jobs on February 24, 1955 in San Francisco, California, the future inventive genius was actually given up for adoption after his birth as his biological parents were a pair of unmarried graduate students and did not want a family right then. He was adopted at birth by Clara and Paul Jobs and the family later moved to Mountain View, California where Steve grew up.

Right from his earliest childhood, it was clear that Steve was no ordinary boy—he was extremely quick in learning and eager to explore. In fact he had already learnt to read from Clara before even starting school. As a child, Steve liked nothing better than to help his father tinker with electronics in the family garage—the two would spend hours taking apart and reassembling televisions, radios and stereos.

At school, Steve quickly learnt all that there was in the curriculum and moved way ahead of his classmates. As a result he was often bored and ended up playing pranks on other students. In fourth grade, he was tested and his score turned out to be that of a high-school sophomore level.

Soon Jobs left for Oregon where he enrolled in Reed College to study. But that old restlessness grew stronger and just after six months, he dropped out.

Fascination with Computers

After travelling for seven months which included a trip to India, Jobs zeroed in on what he wanted to do with his life—computers. Describing his reaction to the first computer terminal he laid eyes on, Steve later said. "I fell totally in love with it." In 1970, a mutual friend introduced Jobs to Steve Wozniak and two hit it off right away. They started making a computer, working out of Jobs' garage and in 1976 created Apple I. This was the first modern personal computer from the ordinary person's perspective. Before the existence of Apple, computers were sold not as assembled machines but in kit form.

Soon Wozniak came up with ideas for an improved version and Jobs convinced investors to put in funds for the Apple II. Their joint endeavour in which Jobs created the design and Wozniak focussed on the technology was a huge success and ushered in a new age of personal computers. In 1984, Jobs launched the Macintosh computer and this in turn changed the whole computer industry. It became the first popular computer with GUI. This did away with the need to remember commands and their syntax. With its powerful operating system and its smooth windows and icons as well as a mouse to move between them, one could now control the computer by just pointing and clicking. Furthermore its GUI made possible the creation of programs such as PageMaker and Photoshop—apps that would revolutionize publishing. Then there was its MacPaint software which enabled ordinary computer users to access digital art.

As soon as the personal computer became a familiar fixture, Jobs being the innovator he was, had to do something better. He ended up inventing the iMac in 1998. It was the first legacy-free personal computer which no longer featured floppy disks. Instead of expansion cards, it had provisions for USB connections. Also it was built for easy internet use since Jobs rightly foresaw how enormously popular the internet would become for sharing of information, entertainment, business and communication.

In the meantime, Jobs had also bought the computer graphics division of Lucas Films and this would mark the birth of the world-famous Pixar Animation Studios. Eventually he would go on to invent a whole range of personal devices like the iPod and iPad. Though music lovers across the world already had their walkmans and mp3 players, Jobs went ahead and invented the iPod. the previous devices lacked in aesthetics and convenience, which iPod had in spades. Combined with clever marketing, the iPod soon became the personal music device of choice. Finally came the iTunes store from where users could easily download music too. This the business model with Apple providing the player, the software and the shop went on to rake in millions of dollars for Jobs and his company.

Innovations Galore

But what transformed the technology industry was the iPhone that Jobs announced in January 2007. Jobs designed this as a single device that would integrate the functions of varied devices such as MP3 players, GPS navigators, cameras and even the personal computer with the mobile phone. The individual technologies like icons, touchscreens and gesture control already existed but disparately. What he did was to come up with a sophisticated operating system which would integrate all these capabilities into a single terminal. This was the iPhone operating system which later came known as 'iOS', the operating system that would go on to power the iPhone, iPad and iPod Touch. Most of all, the iPhone's striking good looks ensured that the customer could never go back to the boxy Blackberry or the chunky Nokia. In this way, iPhone became a game changer for the global smartphone market. Finally in 2008, with the launch of iPhone 3G, Jobs propagated the idea of buying smartphone apps from a single central digital store. With the device already fitted with a powerful operating system and great graphics, now the store offered a free software development kit (SDK) which led to a deluge of apps and that continues even now.

But Jobs was still not done. Even after the iPhone swept the market, he began designing a new device and the result was the iPad which was announced on January 27, 2010. This portable tablet became a success mainly on account of its latest iOS operating system as well as its fantastic Apps. Though the original iPad was only available through Apple stores or its website, still it sold a whopping 300,000 units on the very first day. In the meantime Jobs filed patents to safeguard several of iPhone features and in October 2013—after his death—Apple got the right to protect many details of the original iPhone. Thanks to its continuing massive sales across the world, Apple is now the world's richest technology company

Personal Life

As an individual, Jobs touched the highs and lows of a born genius. While he amazed the world with his innovation and creativity, some people also found him obsessive, finicky and difficult to work with. However most employees were extremely loyal because he knew how to motivate them. In public his image acquired also mythical proportion fuelled as it was by reports of

Apple's enormous financial gains as well as his own appearance—indeed the man in round horn rimmed glasses and black turtleneck sweater became an icon for creative success in popular culture.

At the same time Jobs was rather secretive about his personal life. He was married to business executive Laurene Powell, for more than 20 years. The two were married in a small Buddhist ceremony in Yosemite National Park in 1991. The couple had three children—Reed Paul, Erin Sienna, and Eve and the family lived in Woodside, California. In 2003, Jobs was diagnosed with pancreatic cancer and after a long battle with the disease which also included a liver transplant, he finally died of complications on October 5, 2011.

All his inventions and innovations are ample proof of the creative and business whiz that Steve Jobs was. His biggest successes were not inventions from scratch but masterpieces of reinvention as he himself said, "Innovation distinguishes between a leader and a follower."

Fortune magazine named him as the "greatest entrepreneur of our time"—one who not only excelled in coming up with the perfect technology and design but who could tap into what the user wanted and then delivered something far better.

❑

Quotes of Steve Jobs

Advantage

➢ When we see something or any opportunity then we try to take the advantage of it. We have also taken advantage of many such opportunities such as – desktop films, wireless networking and Intel's. Such creative period is there maximum for ten years but if he use it properly than it may prove to be the golden period.

Advertisements

➢ From advertisements people can be made aware. In this business you cannot fool people. The product itself speaks about its qualities.

Aim

➢ I have only one aim behind the establishment of the company and its products. For manufacturing best products it is necessary to have a strong foundation of the company and to have skilled and talented staff to join the company.

On the other side for me the meaning of the company is an uncommon and wonderful invention by men. This is completely intangible. It is very true that for keeping people united you need a structure of both brick and cement. But for us company is an intangible invention which is very powerful.

- Our main aim had been that instead of improving the product again and again we prefer to give it error free at one time. My experience for business had been that we would have to pay for postponing.
- What is the aim of my life? How can I reply to this question? This is personal talk and I don't want to talk about it.

Alto

- In 1979, when I saw an Alto (that had been developed) at Xerox PARC (Palo Alto Research Center). It was as if, all of a sudden, the veil had been lifted from my eyes. It had the mouse and the multiple-font text on the screen, and you realized in an instant that this would appeal to exponentially more people than the Apple II. I'm talking about people who didn't want to learn how to use a computer—they just wanted to use one. You could eliminate a whole layer of what someone had to know in order to take advantage of this tool.

Amazing

- It's rare that you see an artist in his 30s or 40s able to really contribute something amazing.

Android

- I will spend my last dying breath if I need to, and I will spend every penny of Apple's $40 billion in the bank, to right this wrong. I'm going to destroy Android, because it's a stolen product. I'm willing to go to thermonuclear war on this.

Apple

- Apple has been such an ideal company of Silicon Valley that you can imagine. We had grown from a garage with Woz; I have grown up with Silicon Valley. For us Hewlett-Packard was an ideal and w believed that we would also float a company one day.
- Apple has some tremendous assets, but I believe without some attention, the company could, could, could—I'm searching for the right word—could, could die.
- Apple is a small group of people who are artists and care more about their art than they do about almost anything else. It's more important than finding a girlfriend, it's more important. Than cooking a meal, it's more important than joining the Marines, it's more important than whatever. Look at the way artists work. They're not typically the most "balance" people in the world. Now, yes, we have a few workaholics here who are trying to escape other things, of course. But the majority of people out here have made very conscious decisions; they really have.
- Apple really beats to a different drummer. I used to say that Apple should be the Sony of this business, but in reality, I think Apple should be the Apple of this business.
- Apple took the edge off the word 'computer.'
- Apple's iPad is such a product that the company had never made.

- Apple's market share is bigger than BMW's or Mercedes' or Porsche's in the automotive market. What's wrong with being BMW or Mercedes?
- Apple's overall manner of functioning today is that if you want to become something then prove us by becoming goldsmith of computer.
- At Apple we attract a different type of person—a person who doesn't want to wait five or ten years to have someone takes a giant risk on him or her. Someone who really wants to get in a little over his head and make a little dent in the universe. We are aware that we are doing something significant. We're here at the beginning of it and we're able to shape how it goes. Everyone here has the sense that right now is one of those moments when we are influencing the future.
- Bottom line is, I didn't return to Apple to make a fortune. I've been very lucky in my life and already have one. When I was 25, my net worth was $100 million or so. I decided then that I wasn't going to let it ruin my life. There's no way you could ever spend it all, and I don't view wealth as something that validates my intelligence.
- But Apple really beats to a different drummer. I used to say that Apple should be the Sony of this business, but in reality, I think Apple should be the Apple of this business.
- Funny enough, 20 years after we started Apple, there was nobody building computers for people again. You know? They were trying to sell consumers last year's corporate computers. We said, "Well, these are our roots. This is why we're here. The world doesn't need another Dell or Compaq. They need an Apple."
- Getting fired from Apple was the best thing that could have ever happened to me. The heaviness of being successful was replaced by the lightness of being a beginner again. It freed me to enter one of the most creative periods of my life.

- Here in Apple we are a team of capable people. I appointed team cook as the CEO and gave him the responsibility of Mac division. He did wonderful demonstration. I meant some people say that – "Oh God! If some day some bus crashes down Steve Jobs then Apple Company would completely get destroyed." But I want tell you that this is not the case as with Apple in fact all capable and intelligent people are attached and thereby Directors team can appoint anyone as CEO among them. My job is to make top officials more specialized and more expert in their work that they can easily handle their responsibility.
- I didn't return to Apple to make a fortune. I've been very lucky in my life and already have one. When I was 25, my net worth was $100 million or so. I decided then that I wasn't going to let it ruin my life. There's no way you could ever spend it all, and I don't view wealth as something that validates my intelligence.
- I didn't see it then, but it turned out that getting fired from Apple was the best thing that could have ever happened to me. The heaviness of being successful was replaced by the lightness of being a beginner again, less sure about everything. It freed me to enter one of the most creative periods of my life.
- I don't think it's good that Apple's perceived as different. I think it's important that Apple's perceived as much better. If being different is essential to doing that, then we have to do that, but if we can be much better without being different, that'd be fine with me. I want to be much better.
- I feel as though someone has hit me badly in my stomach and have removed out the entire air out. I am only 30 years old and am carving to make new things. I feel that I can make one more fantastic computer but Apple would not give me such an opportunity.

- I feel like somebody just punched me in the stomach and knocked all my wind out. I'm only 30 years old and I want to have a chance to continue creating things. I know I've got at least one more great computer in me. And Apple is not going to give me a chance to do that.
- I get asked a lot why Apple's customers are so loyal. It's not because they belong to the Church of Mac! That's ridiculous. It's because when you buy our products, and three months later you get stuck on something, you quickly figure out (how to get past it). And you think, "Wow, someone over there at Apple actually thought of this!" And then three months later you try to do something you hadn't tried before, and it works, and you think, "Hey, they thought of that, too." And then six months later it happens again. There's almost no product in the world that you have that experience with, but you have it with a Mac.
- I had been imagining selling one lakh computers in a year but this still remains an imagination. Actually when the result comes in front of me they are something else and I say that this is not the truth and the truth is something else. Next year I will complete 10 years of my working career. I have in my life never done any work for more than a year. When we had launched Apple then for me six months was a very long period. Since, the time I have come into my senses my life has moved on like this only. Every year I have faced so many problems and also had many successes. I have also experienced ample of men who made my one day in Apple seem like a year. This way my ten years of Apple are like ten life durations.
- I have been telling many times that in context with business Apple should become like Sony, but the truth is that in this business Apple should only be like Apple.
- I love what we're doing at Apple now, I think it's the best

work that Apple's ever done. But I think all of us on the Mac team point to that as the high point of our careers. It's like the Beatles playing Shea Stadium. We were really working fourteen-to-eighteen-hour days, seven days a week. For, like, two years, three years. That was our life. But we loved it, we were young, and we could do it.

➢ I observed something very early on at Apple, I didn't know how to explain it then, but I've thought about it since. Most things in life, the dynamic range between "average" and the "best" is, at most, two-to-one. If you get into a cab in New York City with the best cab driver, as opposed to the average cab driver, you're probably going to get to your destination with the best cab driver maybe thirty percent faster…Or a CD player, the difference between the best CD player and the average CD player is what? Twenty percent? So two-to-one is a big dynamic range in most of life. In software—and it used to be the case in hardware too—the difference between the average and the best is 50 to one. Maybe one hundred to one. Very few things in life are like this, but what I've been lucky enough to spend my life in is like this.

➢ I returned back to Apple because it is my belief that with the presence of Apple the world could be better. Now the world without Apple cannot be even imagined.

➢ I want to make Apple a great $10 billion company. Apple has the opportunity to set a new example of how great an American corporation can be, sort of an intersection between science and aesthetics. Something happens to companies when they get to be a few million dollars—their souls go away. And that's the biggest thing I'll be measured on: Were we able to grow a $10 billion company that didn't lose its soul?

➢ I was lucky—I found what I loved to do early in life. Woz and I started Apple in my parents' garage when I was 20. We worked hard, and in 10 years, Apple had grown from just the two of us in a garage into a $2 billion company with over 4000 employees.

- I was on one of my fruitarian diets. I had just come back from the apple farm. It sounded fun, spirited, and not intimidating. Apple took the edge off the word "computer." Plus, it would get us ahead of Atari in the phone book.
- I will always be attached with Apple. I wish that in my entire life, my life string should be entangled with the string of Apple in the manner thread is entangled in the cloth of a photo. Some years may go such that when I may not be there, but I will always return back.
- I will always be attacked with Apple. I have always wanted my life to be attached with Apple. May be in between for some years I would be away from it but I would return back. I have tried to keep on doing it this way only. There is no need to take my talks seriously. If you are an actor or a creator then you do not look back but accept your deeds.
- I'll always stay connected with Apple. I hope that throughout my life I'll sort of have the thread of my life and the thread of Apple weave in and out of each other, like a tapestry. There may be a few years when I'm not there, but I'll always come back.
- If Apple makes such a place that people forget about computers then I would feel that I have lost Apple. But if I live miles apart and still people continue like before at the time of the manufacture of computers then I would think that I have been kept alive.
- If Apple's identity has to be described then it is through its iPad. In this product Apple's mixture of its invention and great design can be seen. Seeing this we can tell that we make such types of things. If anyone will ask me that on the earth what is the status of Apple then I would like to show him the iPad.

- If there was ever a product that catalyzed what's Apple's reason for being, it's this. Because it combines Apple's incredible technology base with Apple's legendary ease of use with Apple's awesome design…it's like, this is what we do. So if anybody was ever wondering why is Apple on the earth, I would hold this up as a good example.
- I'll always stay connected with Apple. I hope that throughout my life I'll sort of have the thread of my life and the thread of Apple weave in and out of each other, like a tapestry. There may be a few years when I'm not there, but I'll always come back.
- In Apple 25, 000 people are working and out of them 10, 000 people are working in the stores. My job is to move along with the 100 employees' together and work with them. This does not mean that all are the Vice President's of the company. Out of these 100 people some are mere technical specialists. Whenever I get a new idea then I rake an opinion about the idea from everyone and at the same time I also argue with those 100 people about the new idea in order to understand how different people look upon it and in this manner only research work can be done.
- In Apple people work for 18 hours. We keep with ourselves people of different nature. Among them some are such people who don't want to wait for 5 to 10 years to know if the company wants to take the risk of keeping them. Such people want to make a place in the world through their talents. We are here from the beginning and so know how to divert things. Every person presents here thinks that the present time is such that with it we can influence the world and the future.
- It's not about charisma and personality, it's about results and products and those very bedrock things that are why people at Apple and outside of Apple are getting more excited

about the company and what Apple stands for and what its potential is to contribute to the industry.

- It's not about charisma and personality, it's about results and products and those very bedrock things that are why people at Apple and outside of Apple are getting more excited about the company and what Apple stands for and what its potential is to contribute to the industry.'
- John Sculley ruined Apple and he ruined it by bringing a set of values to the top of Apple which were corrupt and corrupted some of the top people who were there, drove out some of the ones who were not corruptible, and brought in more corrupt ones and paid themselves collectively tens of millions of dollars and cared more about their own glory and wealth than they did about what built Apple in the first place—which was making great computers for people to use.
- Mostly the business world has been using Macintosh since ten years. Now the time for new invention has come and who can do better invention than Apple? Apple alone has been taking care of the business world by – first Apple II, then Macintosh and LaserWriter. Today also I have special attachment in my heart towards Apple and so would it remain forever.
- So if Apple just becomes a place where computers are a commodity item and where the romance is gone, and where people forget that computers are the most incredible invention that man has ever invented, then I'll feel I have lost Apple. But if I'm a million miles away and all those people still feel those things and they're still working to make the next great personal computer, then I will feel that my genes are still in there.
- The cure for Apple is not cost cutting. The cure for Apple is to innovate its way out of its current predicament.

- They'll want to do what's best for Apple, not what's best for them, what's best for Steve, or anybody else.
- We've got 25,000 people at Apple. About 10,000 of them are in the stores. And my job is to work with sort of the top 100 people, that's what I do. That doesn't mean they're all vice presidents. Some of them are just key individual contributors. So when a good idea comes, you know, part of my job is to move it around, just see what different people think, get people talking about it, argue with people about it, get ideas moving among that group of 100 people, get different people together to explore different aspects of it quietly, and, you know, just explore things.
- We've got really capable people at Apple. I made Tim Cook the COO and gave him the Mac division and he's done brilliantly. I mean, some people say, "Oh, God, if (Jobs) got run over by a bus, Apple would be in trouble." And, you know, I think it wouldn't be a party, but there are really capable people at Apple. And the board would have some good choices about who to pick as CEO. My job is to make the whole executive team good enough to be successors, so that's what I try to do.
- We've never worried about numbers. In the market place, Apple is trying to focus the spotlight on products, because products really make a difference. Good PR educates people; that's all it is. You can't con people in this business. The products speak for themselves.
- Well, Apple invented the PC as we know it, and then it invented the graphical user interface as we know it eight years later (with the introduction of the Mac). But then, the company had a decade in which it took a nap.
- What is Apple, after all? Apple is about people who think 'outside the box, ' people who want to use computers to help

them change the world, to help them create things that make a difference, and not just to get a job done.

- What we are doing here at Apple, I like it and find it to be the best work at Apple. For our career introduction of MAC was as good as climbing Mount Everest. The way Beetles had presented their program in the show stadium, the similar sort experience even we had it. We had daily worked for fourteen to eighteen hours, seven days a week for two to three years continuously. This only has become our life. We liked to do so and could do it as we were young.
- What we do at Apple is very simple: we invent stuff...We make stuff, put it out there, and people use it.

Approach

- So that's our approach. Very simple, and we're really shooting for Museum of Modern Art quality. The way we're running the company, the product design, the advertising, it all comes down to this: Let's make it simple. Really simple.

Artist

- I sat in a garage and invented the future because artists lead and hacks ask for a show of hands!
- If you want to live your life in a creative way, as an artist, you have to not look back too much. You have to be willing to take whatever you've done and whoever you were and throw them away. The more the outside world tries to reinforce an image of you, the harder it is to continue to be an artist, which is why a lot of times, artists have to say, "Bye. I have to go. I'm going crazy and I'm getting out of here." And they go and hibernate somewhere. Maybe later they re-emerge a little differently.

- One such time comes when an artist has to think about his future and if he takes risks then he remains an artist only. Deacon and Picasso always took risks considering their future. Apple is also becoming a risk in my life. It is true that I don't want to be unsuccessful. It might have been that I had to pass many bad experiences but I didn't tell them out until I had thought upon them. I decided that I should not be bothered as this is the job I wanted to do. Even if I am unsuccessful after trying all that I could I would be satisfied that I did all that I could on my part. When you fear of losing something, it is at that moment when you get puzzles. In the book, *Whole Earth* Catalog, on the last page there is a photo of a road of a village. This was a beautiful picture and the title that was printed below it impressed me a lot, it was written – Stay hungry, Stay foolish. This was not an advertisement but a great message of Stewart Brand. The message was – Stay hungry, Stay foolish.
- Picasso had a saying: 'Good artists copy, great artists steal.' We have always been shameless about stealing great ideas...I think part of what made the Macintosh great was that the people working on it were musicians, poets, artists, zoologists and historians who also happened to be the best computer scientists in the world.

Atari

- I never worried about money. I grew up in a middle-class family, so I never thought I would starve. And I learned at Atari that I could be an okay engineer, so I always knew I could get by. I was voluntarily poor when I was in college and India, and I lived a pretty simple life even when I was working. So I went from fairly poor, which was wonderful, because I didn't have to worry about money, to being incredibly rich, when I also didn't have to worry about money. I watched people at Apple who made a lot of money and felt they had to live differently. Some of them bought a Rolls-Royce and various houses, each with a house manager and then someone to manage the house managers. Their wives got plastic surgery and turned into these bizarre people. This was not how I wanted to live. It's crazy. I made a promise to myself that I'm not going to let this money ruin my life.

➢ So we went to Atari and said, 'Hey, we've got this amazing thing, even built with some of your parts, and what do you think about funding us? Or we'll give it to you. We just want to do it. Pay our salary; we'll come work for you.' And they said, 'No.' So then we went to Hewlett-Packard, and they said, 'Hey, we don't need you. You haven't got through college yet.

Atmosphere

➢ The kind of atmosphere we have created then expectations can be done only according to that. My contribution is that I would always emphasize on producing best products.

❑

Bach

- I had been listening to a lot of Bach. All of a sudden the whole field was playing Bach. It was the most wonderful feeling of my life up to that point. I felt like the conductor of this symphony with Bach coming through the wheat. (Regarding using LSD in his youth with his girlfriend in a wheat field outside Sunnyvale).

Belief

- This is not the matter of having a belief in technology; rather it is the matter of having a belief in the customers.
- We had a fundamental belief that doing it right the first time was going to be easier than having to go back and fix it. And I cannot say strongly enough that the repercussions of that attitude are staggering. I've seen them again and again throughout my business life.

Believe

- I believe life is an intelligent thing: those things aren't random.

- I believe that death is the greatest thing as it erases series of old things. I take Apple as a challenge. If tow youngsters come to us with some gadget then will we be able to say it's great? Are we ready to leave away old things? I believe we are because we are aware of considering this.
- I believe that giving away a dollar to anyone is much difficult task than earning a dollar.
- I believe that while trying to make something when you make a good product then you shouldn't sit with it instead try to make another product or achieve another goal.
- I can be very intense in my convictions. And I don't know; all in all, I kind of like myself and I'm not that anxious to change.

Believer

- I'm a big believer in boredom. Boredom allows one to indulge in curiosity and out of curiosity comes everything. All the (technology) stuff is wonderful, but having nothing to do can be wonderful, too.

Bell

- Did Alexander Graham Bell done any market research before he invented the telephone?

Bigger

- We don't know where it will lead. We just know there's something much bigger than any of us here.
- We even don't know where this will take us away. We only know this much that something such should that is much bigger than us all.

Bill Gates

- Bill Gates is a broader guy if he had dropped acid once or gone off to an ashram when he was younger.
- Bill Gates is basically unimaginative and has never invented anything, which is why I think he's more comfortable now in philanthropy than technology. He just shamelessly ripped off other people's ideas.
- I've read something that Bill Gates said. He said, "I worked really, really hard in my 20s." And I know what he means, because I worked really, really hard in my 20s too. Literally, you know, 7 days a week, a lot of hours every day. And it actually is a wonderful thing to do, because you can get a lot done. But you can't do it forever, and you don't want to do it forever, and you have to come up with ways of figuring out what the most important things are and working with other people even more.
- If Bill Gates had spent his youth days in ashram than for sure he would have been more open minded.

Black

- I need it to go black, real black. Get rid of the exit signs, and don't let me know how you did it.

Book

- I have always kept on thinking of making a smart book which one can carry with him anywhere.
- On vacation recently I was reading this book by (physicist and Nobel laureate) Feynman Richard. He had cancer, you know. In this book he was describing one of his last operations before he died. The doctor said to him, "Look, Richard, I'm not sure you're going to make it." And Feynmann made the

doctor promise that if it became clear he wasn't going to survive, to take away the anesthetic. Do you know why? Feynmann said, "I want to feel what it's like to turn off." That's a good way to put yourself in the present—to look at what's affecting you right now and be curious about it even if it's bad.

- Recently, during vacations, I have read a book of a noble prize winner – Feyman's Richard book. He had cancer, in this book he has written about his life's last days before his death. The doctor had told him that he is not sure if he could be saved or not. At this he replied that he thinks that his life cannot be saved and so he should take away the anesthetics also. Why did he say so and what did he mean? Foeman meant that he wanted to feel how death is. This is the best way to face the present. In conclusion to this, we should accept what is happening to us and also, be excited about it even if it is something bad happening to us.

Books and Music

- My favorite things of life are books and music. Things that I love, for them I need not spend money. This is very clear that the most precious thing that we have in life is our own time and I cannot take out time from my personal life to utilize it. I don't have time to build up love relations and sit in a café or eat a tomato and mozzarella salad in Italy. Generally for saving time I spend money. I have purchased an apartment in New York because I love this city. I am trying to educate myself because I have grown up in California which is a small city and so I have remained aloof of the culture and behavior that persists in big cities. I believe this as a part of my education. You know in Apple there are many such people who are kings of their minds and can buy anything to fulfill their desires but still remain rich.

Box

- Even today we are more dependent on the box. We are fond of boxes. Today we have wonderful computers and so are we trying to invent wonderful hardware's. Even today I am engrossed in making new computers and this would only always be Apple's main aim. But we give more importance to the experiences of the users and of those experiences we are spreading away from boxes and for this we are paying attention towards the best use of internet. Customer's experiences are based on four facets – Hardware, Operating system, Applications, and Internet. We want to satisfy our customers in all these four fields.
- I've always thought it would be really wonderful to have a little box, a sort of slate that you could carry along with you.

Builders

- We humans are tool builders. We can fashion tools that amplify the inherent abilities that we have to spectacular magnitudes.

Business

- In our business most of the people do not have different kinds of experience. In fact they do not have so many dots, which they can joint; their thinking on reaching at one said point gets over. They do not understand that there is some alternative solution to that problem. Our design would be best only on having the quality of understanding the experience of man in-depth.
- Throughout the years in business, I found something. I always ask why you do things. The answers you invariably get is, "That's just the way it's done." Nobody knows why

they do what they do. Nobody thinks about things very deeply in business, that's what I found.

Buttons

- We made the buttons on the screen look so good that you'll want to lick them.

❑

Cancer

➢ With the experience of cancer I have got to learn some lessons. I have understood that I love my life. I have a very good family with me and I have important work with me. I like to be engrossed in my work. I do not go in much of the programs. I love my family. I love both Apple and Pixar. I like to direct Apple and in doing so I feel myself to be lucky.

Cannibal

➢ If you don't cannibalize yourself, someone else will.

Career

➢ I don't think of my life as a career. I do stuff. I respond to stuff. That's not a career—it's a life!

Carpenter

➢ When you're a carpenter making a beautiful chest of drawers, you're not going to use a piece of plywood on the back, even though it faces the wall and nobody will see it. You'll know it's there, so you're going to use a beautiful piece of wood on the back. For you to sleep well at night, the aesthetic, the quality, has to be carried all the way through.

Cash

- I hate it when people call themselves "entrepreneurs" when what they're really trying to do is launch a startup and then sell or go public, so they can cash in and move on.

Cent

- I make 50 cents for showing up and the other 50 cents is based on my performance.

CEO

- CEOs are supposed to have class. I can see that isn't an opinion you hold.
- I had wiped off the word interim attached to my post. Today also I am addressed as CEO.

Challenge

- If you don't love something, you're not going to go the extra mile, work the extra weekend, and challenge the status quo as much.

Change

- Interesting thoughts and new inventions change the company, which keeps on discovering new things for many years. For doing all this lots of research and experience both is needed.
- It is not necessary that if anything cannot change the world than it becomes of less importance.

- It's a disservice to constantly put things in this radical new light—that it's going to change everything. Things don't have to change the world to be important.
- Before going to school my mother taught me to study and hence I would get bored in the school. Thus, I became a spoilt child in my third grade and had become a nuisance for my teachers. We would leave snakes in the class or light fire crackers in the classroom itself. In my fourth grade changes came, this change in me was brought about by saint teacher of fourth grade named, Imogene Hill. She had very well understood my problem and thereby created an urge in me to learn more. The things I learnt that year in school were one I had never done.
- I've always been attracted to the more revolutionary changes. I don't know why. Because they're harder. They're much more stressful emotionally. And you usually go through a period where everybody tells you that you've completely failed.
- Things don't have to change the world to be important.
- With our techniques in reality, three people can bring a great change from sitting in the garage itself, where in Microsoft 200 people together do it. There is one very important need of America's corporate sector and with that need lots of money can be made. And if that thing gets missed than so much money will be spent that with that a revolution of new product can be started.

Changing

- While giving speech in the campus when I noted that if a thought that the person giving speech is a millionaire comes in the minds of the students then I feel myself aged. When I studied in the college and there would be people who would come and lecture us then we would be affected by their lectures but now times are changing and students' thinking towards idealness is also changing.

Chip

- There is no odd chip fit on my shoulders for which I need to prove myself to others. My way of looking upon success is different from that of others. My way is that whenever computers have been made they should be the best and should have Macintosh products and machines.

Click

- Click. Boom. Amazing!

Closet

- I don't have any skeletons in my closet that can't be allowed out.

Company

- In the companies where the employee's views are overlooked instead of encouraging then good working atmosphere in the company cannot be formed. By criticizing talented people you start giving importance to average intelligence people. I know this because Apple was launched this way only. Apple Company was formed by employing refuges of different companies. Then the staff comprised of those talented people whom the other companies gave no importance.
- It is hard to think that a $2 billion company with 4, 300-plus people couldn't compete with six people in blue jeans.
- There's no other company that could make a MacBook Air and the reason is that not only do we control the hardware,

but we control the operating system. And it is the intimate interaction between the operating system and the hardware that allows us to do that. There is no intimate interaction between Windows and a Dell notebook.

- A lot of companies have chosen to downsize, and maybe that was the right thing for them. We chose a different path. Our belief was that if we kept putting great products in front of customers, they would continue to open their wallets.
- As a company we always have wished that technology should be reached to more and more people. Doing so we have got happiness. We have done so through Apple-II and now again through Mac we are going to do this. In this century first time dating is taking place between the society and computer and for making this romance successful we are at the right place at the right time.
- Companies, as they grow to become multibillion-dollar entities, somehow lose their vision. They insert lots of layers of middle management between the people running the company and the people doing the work. They no longer have an inherent feel or a passion about the products. The creative people, who are the ones who care passionately, have to persuade five layers of management to do what they know is the right thing to do.
- Generally when a company starts becoming a power of a billion dollar company then it loses its vision. A gap is created between the founders and the employees and thus the enthusiasm for the product is no more left among anyone. A person has to take permission for his invention from five officials.
- I discovered that the best innovation is sometimes the company, the way you organize a company. The whole notion of how you build a company is fascinating.

- I don't believe that work is limited to establish a big company and increase salaries.

Competence

- When I hire somebody really senior, competence is the ante. They have to be really smart. But the real issue for me is, Are they going to fall in love with Apple? Because if they fall in love with Apple, everything else will take care of itself. They'll want to do what's best for Apple, not what's best for them, what's best for Steve, or anybody else.

Computer

- Computer helps people from several complexities. It also enhances people's ability of creation. Always remember computer is a technology and through technology we get means to do our work in a better manner.
- Computers themselves and software yet to be developed will revolutionize the way we learn.
- From most of the personal computer companies engineering is over. Consumer oriented electronic manufacturing companies have no knowledge of the software that is installed in the product. This is the only reason why you cannot make that product. That is made only in Apple. Apple alone is such a company where everything is under one roof.
- In fact no one wants to understand how computers work. Many people don't know how does an automatic transmission work but they know how it to drive the car perfectly. For driving a car you need not learn the principles of speed and for using Macintosh you needn't know the principles or rules.
- It took us three years to build the NeXT computer. If we'd given customers what they said they wanted, we'd have

built a computer they'd have been happy with a year after we spoke to them-not something they'd want now.

- That's what a computer is to me: the computer is the most remarkable tool that we've ever come up with. It's the equivalent of a bicycle for our minds.
- This whole vision of a personal computer just popped into my head. I started to sketch out on paper what would later become known as the Apple I.
- Today we are using computer like an obedient servant. We ask it to prepare a spread sheet, ask it to correct a letter. You find that computer's excellence as a servant cannot be matched with anyone. But now they would play the role of guides and agents.
- We're going to be able to ask our computers to monitor things for us, and when certain conditions happen, are triggered, the computers will take certain actions and inform us after the fact.
- What if the computer was a beautiful object? Something you wanted to look at and have in your home. And what if instead of it being in the right hands, it was in everyone's hands?

Concentration

- We motivate more towards concentration. People think that why is it necessary to be focused on everything. But this actually means to choose one best thought out of millions of good thoughts. I am really proud of that I did not pay attention towards manufacturing of several products, in the same manner as I feel proud on manufacturing some products.

Confused

- People get confused; companies get confused. When they start getting bigger, they want to replicate their initial success. And a lot of them think, "Well, somehow, there's some magic in the process of how that success was created." So they start to institutionalize process across the company. And before very long, people start to get confused that the process is the content. And that's ultimately the downfall of IBM. IBM has the best process people in the world. They just forgot about the content. And that happened a little bit at Apple, too. We had a lot of people who were great at management process. They just didn't have a clue about the content. In my career, I found that the best people are the ones that really understand the content. And they're a pain in the butt to manage! But you put up with it because they're so great at the content. And that's what makes great products. It's not process, it's content.

Context

- I am ambitious, in the context that I believe that people are respectful and sober and out if them some are really capable. My thinking towards people is very ambitious.

Contribution

- My best contribution to the group is not settling for anything but really good stuff. A lot of times, people don't do great things because great things really aren't expected of them, and nobody ever really demands that they try, and nobody says, "Hey, that's the culture here." If you set that up, people will do things that are greater than they ever thought they could be. Really some great work that will go down in history.

- My important contribution for the group is that I always press wise upon making a superior thing. Many a times when we do not keep expectations from people for making great things than they cannot even make it. As no one even demands from them such a thing and nor does tell them, 'Here this kind of work culture is there. 'When you will keep the quality of superior things then such things only make history.

Control

- I always want that whatever we do, on its beginning I should have my ownership and control.
- Pretend to be completely in control and people will assume that you are.

Courage

- Don't let the noise of others' opinions drown out your own inner voice. And most important, have the courage to follow your heart and intuition.
- Have the courage to follow your heart and intuition. They somehow already know what you truly want to become. Everything else is secondary.

Creativity

- Creativity is just connecting things. When you ask creative people how they did something, they feel a little guilty because they didn't really do it, they just saw something. It seemed obvious to them after a while. That's because they were able to connect experiences they've had and synthesize new things. And the reason they were able to do that was that they've had more experiences or they have thought more about their experiences than other people.

Customer

- Customers can't anticipate what the technology can do. They won't ask for things that they think are impossible. But the technology may be ahead of them. If you happen to mention something, they'll say, 'Of course, I'll take that. Do you mean I can have that, too?' It sounds logical to ask customers what they want and then give it to them. But they rarely wind up getting what they really want that way.
- Customers don't know what technology can do for them. The things that they feel impossible, they would not demand that from you. But technology can move ahead of the customers. If you describe any such product to a customer, he would say, "Surely I would buy such a product but do you mean that I can but that too?" saying so sounds double meaning. But this is very rare that you would find a customer knowing well about his likes properly.
- Be early. Stay late. Make the extra phone call. Send the extra email. Do the extra research. Help a customer unload or unpack a shipment.
- I am generally asked that why customers so honest towards Apple are. It is not right to think that they are keeping respect for Mac. It is actually so that when anyone purchases our product and even after three months comes with some problem then it is easily solved. Then you think how people of Apple thought in advance about such problems had. Then after three months you try to do that you have never done in that also you succeed. Then you think that Apple people knew even this. In the world there is no second product which gives you this much satisfaction the way Apple does.
- Some people say, "Give the customers what they want." But that's not my approach. Our job is to figure out what they're going to want before they do. I think Henry Ford once said,

"If I'd asked customers what they wanted, they would have told me, 'A faster horse!'" People don't know what they want until you show it to them. That's why I never rely on market research. Our task is to read things that are not yet on the page.

Customers

- This is what customers pay us for – to sweat all these details so it's easy and pleasant for them to use our computers. We're supposed to be really good at this. That doesn't mean we don't listen to customers, but it's hard for them to tell you what they want when they've never seen anything remotely like it. Take desktop video editing. I never got one request from someone who wanted to edit movies on his computer. Yet now that people see it, they say, 'Oh my God, that's great!'

❑

Dacoit

- When you can become a dacoit of the sea then what's the need of going in the ship.

Day

- I have always said if there ever came a day when I could no longer meet my duties.

Death

- Death is very likely the single best invention of Life.
- Keep this thing in mind that I will die very soon, this helps me taking big decisions in my life; because once when I think about death then my hopes, all ego and the fear of failure all disappears and only those things remain that are actually needed. Remember one thing that one day we have to die this thought is the best way to keep us away from the fear of losing anything. There is no such reason that you do not listen to your heart.
- No one wants to die. Even people who want to go to heaven don't want to die to get there. And yet death is the destination we all share. No one has ever escaped it. And that is as

it should be, because Death is very likely the single best invention of Life. It is Life's change agent. It clears out the old to make way for the new. Right now the new is you, but someday not too long from now, you will gradually become the old and be cleared away. Sorry to be so dramatic, but it is quite true.

- Probably death alone is the biggest invention of this life.

Decide

- Deciding what not to do is as important as deciding what to do.

Decision

- You can ask that how are decision related to skills taken? There are several such things, for example – a good car's all qualities are taken into consideration from the ground level itself. I feel that electronics is also based on quality. I have seen that successful companies pay special attention towards quality. They use most of their time in making the product trustworthy. This attitude brings positive results to the company. I mean that, through the quality of the product, the companies can display the reputation of their company to the world. With the quality we come to know about the discipline that has been followed in the Engineering Department and on what principles is the company functioning.

Design

- Design is a funny word. Some people think design means how it looks. But of course, if you dig deeper, it's really how it works. The design of the Mac wasn't what it looked like, although that was part of it. Primarily, it was how it worked. To design something really well, you have to get it. You have to really grok what it's all about. It takes a passionate commitment to really thoroughly understand something, chew it up, and not just quickly swallow it. Most people don't take the time to do that.

- Design is not just what it looks like and feels like. Design is how it works.
- Design is not that shows the appearance of the product or how does it feels, rather design is how does the product works.
- Design is the fundamental soul of a man-made creation that ends up expressing itself in successive outer layers of the product or service. The iMac is not just the color or translucence or the shape of the shell. The essence of the iMac is to be the finest possible consumer computer in which each element plays together.
- It's really hard to design products by focus groups. A lot of times, people don't know what they want until you show it to them. That doesn't mean we don't listen to customers, but it's hard for them to tell you what they want when they've never seen anything remotely like it.
- It's really hard to design products by focus groups. A lot of times, people don't know what they want until you show it to them.
- Look at the design of a lot of consumer products—they're really complicated surfaces. We tried to make something much more holistic and simple. When you first start off trying to solve a problem, the first solutions you come up with are very complex, and most people stop there. But if you keep going, and live with the problem and peel more layers of the onion off, you can often times arrive at some very elegant and simple solutions. Most people just don't put

in the time or energy to get there. We believe that customers are smart, and want objects which are well thought through.

- Macs design was not as it appeared though it was its part's only. Initially it was as it worked. Actually to make a good design you need to go in the depth of it and so also you have to understand the purpose of it. For understanding anything you need to have craze of it, in other words it is no use to swallow a thing rather it should be chewed it properly.
- Mostly the meaning of the design lies in the words of the people, the outer appearance or the room's decoration or the cloth of the curtain or the fabric covered on the sofa but for me design means only the actual meaning of it nothing else.
- That's not what we think design is. It's not just what it looks like and feels like. Design is how it works.
- The design of the Mac wasn't what it looked like, although that was part of it. Primarily, it was how it worked. To design something really well, you have to get it. You have to really grok what it's all about. It takes a passionate commitment to really thoroughly understand something, chew it up, and not just quickly swallow it.
- The main thing in our design is that we have to make things intuitively obvious.
- We had the hardware expertise, the industrial design expertise and the software expertise, including iTunes. One of the biggest insights we have was that we decided not to try to manage your music library on the iPod, but to manage it in iTunes. Other companies tried to do everything on the device itself and made it so complicated that it was useless.
- For something this complicated, it's really hard to design products by focus groups. A lot of times, people don't know what they want until you show it to them.

Desktop

- Desktop computers by now are coming to an end. Its inventions have also been stopped. Microsoft till date has maintained its importance only of very little inventions. This lesson is over and here Apple has lost. Desk top market has entered into darkness and so will this market remain in darkness for another ten years.
- Desktop was invented because it was only one of its types and also as at that time you required to keep your figures and calculations only with yourself. This was a very big thing for the Desk top world and now its need has come to an end. That day is not far when you will not need to collect anything and keep it.
- The desktop computer industry is dead. Innovation has virtually ceased. Microsoft dominates with very little innovation. That's over. Apple lost. The desktop market has entered the dark ages, and it's going to be in the dark ages for the next 10 years, or certainly for the rest of this decade.
- The desktop metaphor was invented because one, you were a stand-alone device, and two; you had to manage your own storage. That's a very big thing in a desktop world. And that may go away. You may not have to manage your own storage. You may not store much before too long.

Detail

- Details matter, it's worth waiting to get it right.

Difference

- The difference that Jony Ive has made, not only at Apple but in the world, is huge. If I had to pick a spiritual partner at Apple, its Jony.

- What is the difference between Mac – founder of MAC Group and PC Junior founder of IBM. I believe that MAC would have greater sales whereas we have not manufacture MAC through other's point of view but through ours. We had jointly decided that this product would be the best and hence for this we didn't go to nor did we go to any market for survey. We just wanted to make a creative and good product. If you are a carpenter and manufacture a beautiful drawer then you would never use plywood in the back part though that part would always remain attached with the wall with no visibility to anyone. Instead you would use a good and strong hard wood so that you get a good sleep at night. Hence, it is essential to always give priority to the quality.

Difficult

- It is very difficult to design products on considering one special community; because many people do not know what they want until you do not show them.

Discouraged

- What happens in most companies is that you don't keep great people under working environments where individual accomplishment is discouraged rather than encouraged. The great people leave and you end up with mediocrity. I know, because that's how Apple was built. Apple is an Ellis Island company. Apple is built on refugees from other companies. These are the extremely bright individual contributors who were troublemakers at other companies.

Discovery

- New discovery shows the difference between a leader and a follower.

Disease

- Living with a disease like cancer, and all the pain, constantly reminds you of your own mortality, and that can do strange things to your brain if you're not careful. You don't make plans more than a year out, and that's bad. You need to force yourself to plan as if you will live for many years.

DNA

- Our DNA is as a consumer company for that individual customer who's voting thumbs up or thumbs down. That's who we think about. And we think that our job is to take responsibility for the complete user experience. And if it's not up to par, it's our fault, plain and simply.

Dollar

- I'm convinced that to give away a dollar effectively is harder than to make a dollar.

Dot

- I like dots a lot as with the dot, curiosity takes place and with the presence of curiosity takes place and with the presence of curiosity invention takes place.

Dots

- One more thing, you cannot join these dots by looking in front, for joining them you will have to look backwards meaning look into your past time. With this faith in you would developed that, yes! These dots in future would be joined somewhere. You will have to have trust on something like—your inner voice, fate, life, work or anything. This thinking has never allowed me to be disappointed and so has it completely changed my life.

- Unfortunately, that's too rare a commodity. A lot of people in our industry haven't had very diverse experiences. So they don't have enough dots to connect, and they end up with very linear solutions without a broad perspective on the problem. The broader one understands of the human experience, the better design we will have.
- You can't connect the dots looking forward; you can only connect them looking backwards. So you have to trust that the dots will somehow connect in your future. You have to trust in something—your gut, destiny, life, karma, whatever. This approach has never let me down, and it has made all the difference in my life.

Dramatic

- Right now the new is you, but someday not too long from now, you will gradually become the old and be cleared away. Sorry to be so dramatic, but it is quite true.

Dream

- We used to dream about this stuff. Now we get to build it. It's pretty great.

❑

Emphasized

- When we were preparing operating systems then we had emphasized on how it has to be made easy and powerful.

Engineering

- The engineering is long gone in most PC companies. In the consumer electronics companies, they don't understand the software parts of it. And so you really can't make the products that you can make at Apple anywhere else right now. Apple's the only company that has everything under one roof.

Enthusiastic

- We're just enthusiastic about what we do.

Every

- Every once in a while a revolutionary product comes along that changes everything. One is very fortunate if you get to work on just one of these in your career. Apple's been very fortunate it's been able to introduce a few of these into the world.

- Every once in a while a revolutionary product comes along that changes everything. One is very fortunate if you get to work on just one of these in your career. Apple's been very fortunate it's been able to introduce a few of these into the world.
- Every time you do something, think of one extra thing you can do…especially if other people aren't doing that extra thing.

Everyone

- On individual basis everyone is good from inside. But when I see people on the basis of a group then my opinion becomes negative and then when I see what is happening in our country then I become worried, whereas this country is the merriest making country of the world. We do not seem to be excited about making our country a better place for our children.
- Everyone here has the sense that right now is one of those moments when we are influencing the future.
- Everyone, everyone, everyone. Everyone is waiting for the Mac.

Experience

- Taking LSD was a profound experience, one of the most important things in my life. LSD shows you that there's another side to the coin, and you can't remember it when it wears off, but you know it. It reinforced my sense of what was important, creating great things instead of making money, putting things back into the stream of history and of human consciousness as much as I could.
- When you open the box of an iPhone or iPad, we want that tactile experience to set the tone for how you perceive the product.

- If you're going to make connections which are innovative... you have to not have the same bag of experiences as everyone else does.
- My generation wanted to more richly experience why were we were alive, not just make a better life, and so people went in search of things. The great thing that came from those that time was to realize that there was definitely more to life than the materialism of the late 50s and early 60s. We were going in search of something deeper.

Experiences

- When these start-ups sell out, even though they get fabulously rich, they're gapping themselves out of one of the potentially most rewarding experiences of their unfolding lives. Without it, they may never know their values or how to keep their new-found wealth in perspective.
- When they will sell their products then they will become rich doing so, yet they will feel themselves being left out in their life by not being able to experiencing life of a rich man. Without this they would not be able to understand their own value and nor would they understand as to how should they look upon their own income.

Expert

- I am expert at finding talented people and then grouping them. I respect the direction in which Apple is going but personally I take interest in making new products. If I cannot make new products at a place then I keep on searching for such options.

❑

Faith

- I think this is a natural feeling in an orphan to search for their roots but I have been keeping my faith on my surroundings. I strongly believe that the manner in which you have been brought by and the culture and teachings that are in your blood make the base on which your personality is developed. But still some things are different towards which emotions are natural to be developed.
- It is not the talk of having faith on the tools with which you are working. Tools are only tools as either they work or they do not work. In fact actually these are only people on whom either you have faith or not. Yes! Even now I am ambitious, I mean that many a times I too get disappointed but not for too long.
- It's not a faith in technology. It's faith in people.
- It's not the tools that you have faith in-tools are just tools. They work, or they don't work. It's people you have faith in or not. Yeah, sure, I'm still optimistic I mean, I get pessimistic sometimes but not for long.

Father

➢ My father was a machinist, and he was a sort of genius with his hands. He can fix anything and make it work and take any mechanical thing apart and get it back together. That was my first glimpse of it. I started to gravitate more toward electronics, and he used to get me things I could take apart and put back together.

Figure

➢ I think if you do something and it turns out pretty good, then you should go do something else wonderful, not dwell on it for too long. Just figure out what's next.

Find

➢ I end up not buying a lot of things, because I find them ridiculous.

Fire

➢ If a fire causes a stampede to the unmarked exits, it will have been well worth it for those who survive. For those who don't, less so, but still pretty good.

Focus

➢ That's been one of my mantras—focus and simplicity. Simple can be harder than complex: You have to work hard to get your thinking clean to make it simple. But it's worth it in the end because once you get there, you can move mountains.

➢ We tend to focus much more. People think focus means saying yes to the thing you've got to focus on. But that's not what it means at all. It means saying no to the hundred other good ideas that there are. You have to pick carefully. I'm actually as proud of many of the things we haven't done as the things we have done.

Foundation

- I have always wished that whatever we do, we should have control on all its technical foundation.

Future

- The best way to predict the future is to invent it.

❑

Generation

- One generation instead of spending better life was interested in more understanding the definition no better life and so we were in search of balance. We tried to understand those experiences that was beyond the 50s and 60s people had experienced. We wanted to go more in depth and know the truth.

Give Up

- There are such rough moments in time that I think most people give up. I don't blame them. It's really tough and it consumes your life. If you've got a family and you're in the early days of a company, I can't imagine how one could do it. I'm sure it's been done but it's rough. It's pretty much an 18-hour day job, seven days a week for a while. Unless you have a lot of passion about this, you're not going to survive.

Goal

- Our goal is to make the best devices in the world, not to be the biggest.

God

- God sent his only son on a suicide mission, but people like him because he made trees.
- I have seen a video tape which we have not criticized for watching. It was prepared by an Army Chief Officer. Seeing this tape we came to know that a few years back in Europe every nuclear weapon was kept under aim through Apple Computers. The good thing in is that in computers TIS is not present and for this we should thank God.
- I mean, some people say, 'Oh, God, if Jobs got run over by a bus, Apple would be in trouble.' And, you know, I think it wouldn't be a party, but there are really capable people at Apple. My job is to make the whole executive team good enough to be successors, so that's what I try to do.
- I saw a video tape that we weren't supposed to see. It was prepared for the Joint Chiefs of Staff. By watching the tape, we discovered that, at least as of a few years ago, every tactical nuclear weapon in Europe manned by U.S personnel was targeted by an Apple II computer. Now, we didn't sell computers to the military; they went out and bought them at a dealer's, I guess. But it didn't make us feel good to know that our computers were being used to target nuclear weapons in Europe. The only bright side of it was that at least they weren't Radio Shack TRS-80s! Thank God for that.
- Sometimes I believe in God, sometimes I don't. I think it's 50-50 maybe. But ever since I've had cancer, I've been thinking about it more. And I find myself believing a bit more. I kind of—maybe it's 'cause I want to believe in an afterlife. That when you die, it doesn't just all disappear. The wisdom you've accumulated. Somehow it lives on, but sometimes I think it's just like an on-off switch. Click

and you're gone. And that's why I don't like putting on-off switches on Apple devices.

Greatest Thing

- The greatest thing is when you do put your heart and soul into something over an extended period of time, and it is worth it.

Grow Up

- When you grow up you tend to get told the world is the way it is and to live your life inside the world. Try not to bash into the walls too much. Try to have a nice family, have fun, save a little money. That's a very limited life. Life can be much broader once you discover one simple fact: Everything around you that you call life was made up by people that were no smarter than you and you can change it, you can influence it, and you can build your own things that other people can use. Once you learn that, you'll never be the same again.

❑

Harder

- Simple can be harder than complex: You have to work hard to get your thinking clean to make it simple. But it's worth it in the end because once you get there, you can move mountains.
- When we laid some people off at Apple a year ago, or when I have to take people out of their jobs, it's harder for me now. Much harder. I do it because that's my job. But when I look at people when this happens, I also think of them as being 5 years old. And I think that person could be me coming home to tell my wife and kids that I just got laid off. Or that could be one of my kids in 20 years. I never took it so personally before. Life is short, and we're all going to die really soon.

Here

- We're here to put a dent in the universe. Otherwise why else even be here?

History

- It will go down in history as a turning point for the music industry. This is landmark stuff. I can't overestimate it!

Honest

- I'm brutally honest, because the price of admission to being in the room with me is I get to tell you you're full of shit if you're full of shit, and you get to say to me I'm full of shit, and we have some rip-roaring fights. And that keeps the B-players, the bozos, from larding the organization. Only the A-players survive. And the people who do survive, say, "Yeah, he was rough." They say things even worse than "He cut in line in front of me, " but they say, "This was the greatest ride I've ever had, and I would not give it up for anything."

Human

- I'm an optimist in the sense that I believe humans are noble and honorable, and some of them are really smart. I have a very optimistic view of individuals.

❑

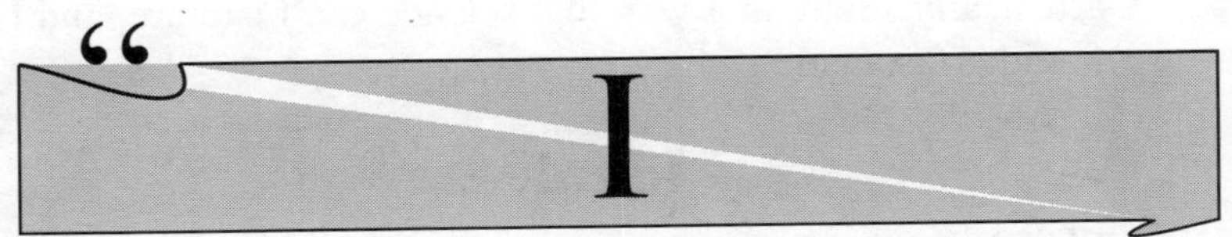

IBM

- It's like when IBM drove a lot of innovation out of the computer industry before the microprocessor came along. Eventually, Microsoft will crumble because of complacency, and maybe some new things will grow. But until that happens, until there's some fundamental technology shift, it's just over.
- If, for some reason, we make some big mistake and IBM wins, my personal feeling is that we are going to enter a computer Dark Ages for about twenty years.

Idea

- But newness comes from those people who meet in the galleries that reach till the hall or from those people who talk in the night at 10:30 with one another on the phone discussing about some new idea or they speak regarding some deficiencies that were coming in between their thinking towards the achievement of solution.
- I had no idea what I wanted to do with my life and no idea how college was going to help me figure it out. And here I was spending all of the money my parents had saved their entire life. So I decided to drop out and trust that it would all

work out okay…The minute I dropped out I began dropping in on the classes that looked interesting. I learned about serif and sans serif typefaces, about varying the amount of space between different letter combinations, about what makes great typography great. It was beautiful, historical, artistically subtle in a way that science can't capture, and I found it fascinating.

Ideal

- My ideal hero David Packard left his all wealth with his foundation. Intel's co-establisher, Noyce, all did this. It is my good luck that I know such people. When I was 21 years old, I met Andy Grove and told him that no one can do operations like him and asked him to accompany me for lunch. I had done the same with others also that I met. The atmosphere at Silicon Valley deeply affected me. There were many such people also who ran their companies only to earn money but were unsuccessful in establishing great companies.
- The time when I had started this my age was 20 or 21 years. My ideal was Intel's Robert Noyce who worked in semi conductor field, Andy Grove and Bill Hewlett and David Packard. These were all such people who did not wanted to earn money alone but they wanted to change the world and so did they wanted to establish such companies which achieves more and more success and brings changes. They have today left heritages behind them. Only opening companies and selling their shares was not important. It is like the role of mother and father how they feel good keeping their children with them.

Identity

- My self-identity does not revolve around being a businessman, though I recognize that is what I do. I think of myself more as a person who builds neat things. I like building neat things. I like making tools that are useful to people. I like working with very bright people. I like interacting in the world of ideas, though somehow those ideas have to be tied to some physical reality. One of the things I like the most is dropping a new idea on a bunch of incredibly smart and talented people and then letting them work it out themselves. I like all of that very, very much.

iMac

- In most people's vocabularies, design means veneer. It's interior decorating. It's the fabric of the curtains and the sofa. But to me, nothing could be further from the meaning of design. Design is the fundamental soul of a man-made creation that ends up expressing itself in successive outer layers of the product or service. The iMac is not just the color or translucence or the shape of the shell. The essence of the iMac is to be the finest possible consumer computer in which each element plays together. On our latest iMac, I was adamant that we get rid of the fan, because it is much more pleasant to work on a computer that doesn't drone all the time. That was not just 'Steve's decision' to pull out the fan; it required an enormous engineering effort to figure out how to manage power better and do a better job of thermal conduction through the machine. That is the furthest thing from veneer. It was at the core of the product the day we started.
- When people look at iMac then they like the design a lot. Mostly people go for outward beauty. After iMac's launching in the market then for two years it had not been possible for anyone to copy it and make it. This is the matter to see that the specialized engineering that was used for making it was great. This is my same opinion for cube and other products.

- When people see iMac then they say that we can produce products to show the right direction to the people globally. This is not the case of magic or miracles; rather it is only the case of best products and hard work. This is the only reason why people in Apple and outside are seemed very excited taking Apple Company.

Important

- Most important thing is your trust on the people. If you give them device then they would use them in a better way. You should not have faith only on the devices as they may work or not but you should always have faith on the people. It is true that even today I am ambitious and in between I too get depressed.

Industry

- Many times people tell me that you are working with 'world's speedy industry' but I don't feel so. I in fact believe that I am working with a low speed industry because for the outcomes of anything it takes years.

Innovate

- To turn really interesting ideas and fledgling technologies into a company that can continue to innovate for years, it requires a lot of disciplines.

Innovation

- Pretty much, Apple and Dell are the only ones in this industry making money. They make it by being Walmart. We make it by innovation.
- But innovation comes from people meeting up in the hallways or calling each other at 10:30 at night with a new

idea, or because they realized something that shoots holes in how we've been thinking about a problem. Its ad hoc meetings of six people called by someone who thinks he has figured out the coolest new thing ever and who wants to know what other people think of his idea.

- Innovation distinguishes between a leader and a follower.
- Innovation has nothing to do with how many R & D dollars you have. When Apple came up with the Mac, IBM was spending at least 100 times more on R & D. It's not about money. It's about the people you have, how you're led, and how much you get it.

Internet

- Internet is not a new thing and it has been here since 10 years. Now a common computer operator has started liking it and that is what I like. I feel attracted towards a cave in comparison to a drawing room. To make internet reach to houses means to use telecom communication. This is not like making a set up box digital. With this at the most video rental shop would be closed and for seeing a film we need not go outside. I am not excited taking this point and nor am I excited with home shopping. I am only excited about the internet in my cave.
- It's hard to tell with these Internet startups if they're really interested in building companies or if they're just interested in the money. I can tell you, though: If they don't really want to build a company, they won't luck into it. That's because it's so hard that if you don't have a passion, you'll give up.
- It's hard to tell with these Internet startups if they're really interested in building companies or if they're just interested

in the money. I can tell you, though: If they don't really want to build a company, they won't luck into it. That's because it's so hard that if you don't have a passion, you'll give up.

- I stay very enthusiastic for the internet being in my room.
- I'm very excited about having the Internet in my den.
- I've seen the demonstrations on the Internet about how you can find another person using a Zune and give them a song they can play three times. It takes forever. By the time you've gone through all that, the girl's got up and left! You're much better off to take one of your ear buds out and put it in her ear. Then you're connected with about two feet of headphone cable.
- What's new is this amazingly efficient distribution system for stolen property called the Internet and no one's going to shut down the Internet.

Intuition

- We didn't know much about each other twenty years ago. We were guided by our intuition; you swept me off my feet. It was snowing when we got married at the Ahwahnee. Years passed, kids came, good times, hard times, but never bad times. Our love and respect has endured and grown. We've been through so much together and here we are right back where we started twenty years ago—older, wiser—with wrinkles on our faces and hearts. We now know many of life's joys, sufferings, secrets and wonders and we're still here together. My feet have never returned to the ground.

Invent

- Let's go invent tomorrow instead of worrying about what happened yesterday.

Inventing

- We are inventing the future. Think about surfing on the front edge of a wave. It's really exhilarating. Now think about dog-paddling at the tail end of that wave. It wouldn't be anywhere near as much fun. Come down here and make a dent in the universe.

Invention

- From the invention it becomes clear that who is the leader and who is the follower.
- Invention does not mean how many dollars are there with you. When Apple made MAC at that time IBM was spending more money on Research and Development. This does not mean how much money you have, it actually means. What kind of people you have, what style of leadership do you follow and what do you want to achieve.
- Inventions do not mean the amount of money there is in your purse. When Apple had made Mac that time IBM in comparison to Apple was spending 100 times to them in the process of launching computer. This matter has no relation with money as it only depends on the kind of people are there with you. How your outlook is and what do you want to achieve?

Inventions

- Of all the inventions of humans, the computer is going to rank near or at the top as history unfolds and we look back. It is the most awesome tool that we have ever invented. I feel incredibly lucky to be at exactly the right place in Silicon Valley, at exactly the right time, historically, where this invention has taken form.

iPhone

- An iPod, a phone, an internet mobile communicator... these are NOT three separate devices! And we are calling it iPhone! Today Apple is going to reinvent the phone. And here it is.
- I think right now it's a battle for the mindshare of developers and for the mindshare of customers, and right now iPhone and Android are winning that battle.
- One Ipad, one phone, and one internet, i.e. mobile messenger-all these three are not different technologies and we call them iphone. Today Apple is again going to give a new appearance to phone and so has it come also.

iPod

- We made the iPod for ourselves, and when you're doing something for yourself, or your best friend or family, you're not going to cheese out. If you don't love something, you're not going to go the extra mile, work the extra weekend, and challenge the status quo as much.
- I am very fortunate that when I was growing up then I could understand the importance of singing. At that time singing would affect the children also and it did the same to me too. I know for sometime the importance of singing had faded. IPod's music had again made music an integral part of people's life. I feel very good and relaxed seeing the change that iPod has brought about in people's life. I believe that music is important for the soul too.

iTunes

- We put iTunes on Windows in order to sell more iPods. But I don't see an advantage of putting our music app on Android, except to make Android users happy. And I don't want to make Android users happy.

❑

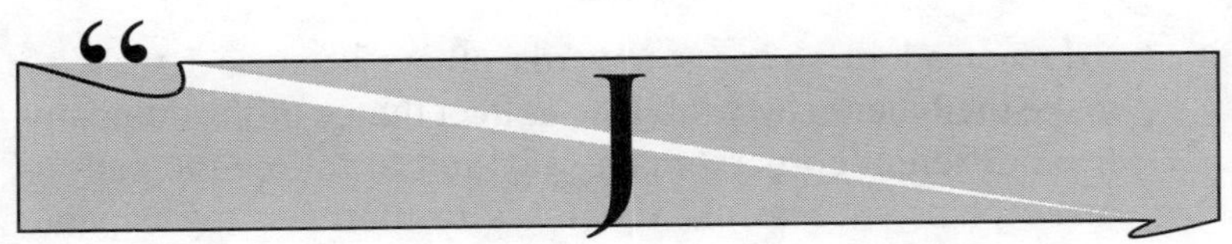

Japan

- Japan is really interesting. Some people think that Japanese copy things but I don't think so. I believe that these people invent a thing in a complete new manner. Whenever they get a new thing they study and research about it until they understand it completely. At times they accumulate the knowledge of products more and then it is manufactured. They understand that product and once when they are done with it they make the product in anew manner. This can be done only when the product is not completely changed. Stereo and automobiles industry can be considered an appropriate example in this context. If there are changed is the product's speedily then it becomes very difficult for them as to make a new product it takes a long time maybe several years. The speed in which the computers are changing it would not be easy for the Japanese to copy it.
- Japan's tech companies are very interesting. Some people think it copies things. I don't think that anymore. I think what they do is reinvent things. They will get something that's already been invented and study it until they thoroughly understand it. In some cases, they understand it better than the original inventor.

Japanese

- The Japanese have hit the shores like dead fish. They're just like dead fish washing up on the shores.

Job

- I do not adopt softness towards others because I want to make them better. My job is to collect things of the company from different corners, make way and to follow the path to make plans successful. My job is to motivate my capable works and make them more polished in order to increase their intelligence.
- I our workers are working in such an atmosphere where inquisitiveness is criticized then he can do a job on his own with his self – inquisitiveness. I am talking of such an atmosphere where inquisitiveness is seen and curiosity is respected. If there is such an atmosphere then you don't need to force anyone to take up such jobs as people understand themselves with their surroundings.
- It is no sense of being a richest dead body of the crematory. To tell myself in the night while sleeping that I have done wonderful job, for me this is the most important thing.
- My job is not to be easy on people. My job is to make them better.
- My job is to pull things together from different parts of the company and clear the ways and get the resources for the key projects. And to take these great people we have and to push them and make them even better, coming up with more aggressive visions of how it could be.
- My job is to say when something sucks rather than sugarcoat it.
- So when a good idea comes, you know, part of my job is to move it around, just see what different people think,

get people talking about it, argue with people about it, get ideas moving among that group of 100 people, get different people together to explore different aspects of it quietly, and, you know—just explore things.

- To appoint workers is a difficult job. It is as difficult as finding out needle from the lump of the waste. We do this job ourselves and doing so it takes a long time. I have in my life participated in more than 5000 people's interview. Therefore I do this work with great seriousness. As you cannot know everything in an hour's interview period. In the end all this depends on your judgment. How do I like the opposite person? How can he behave at the time of problems? He has come here for doing what? This I used to ask generally to everyone. With the reply to this question I was able to understand whether he is the kind of person I am searching.

Join

- It's better to be a pirate than to join the navy.

Journey

- The journey is the reward.

❑

Lead

- And no, we don't know where it will lead. We just know there's something much bigger than any of us here.

Learn

- I've learned over the years that when you have really good people you don't have to baby them. By expecting them to do great things, you can get them to do great things. The original Mac team taught me that A-plus players like to work together, and they don't like it if you tolerate B work.

Life

- If you want to live your life in a creative way, as an artist, you have to not look back too much. You have to be willing to take whatever you've done and whoever you were and throw them away.
- In life many times we regret after doing several jobs, like you liked a girl and you couldn't ask her to dance. In business, till what I know, if I would had known before then I would preferred some jobs in a more better way. But it could also have happened that I would have done some jobs in a more

bad way. Hence, to live in present is only most important thing.

- In my life my favorite works are those for which I do not need money. The most precious thing that we all have with us is time.
- Do you want to spend the rest of your life selling sugared water or do you want a chance to change the world?
- I didn't new that my life would be like this. I stay in Apple for some time and then come out and make something new but I would still remain attached with Apple and so would return back. After returning I would stay back for a long time and then again come out and work. But the way I had thought it is not working like that. I have passed ten best years of my life and I don't have any regret.
- I don't think much about my time of life. I just get up in the morning and it's a new day. Somebody told me when I was 17 to live each day as if it were my last, and that one day I'd be right. I am at a stage where I don't have to do things just to get by. But then I've always been that way because I've never really cared about money that much. I guess what I'm trying to say is that I feel the same way now as I felt when I was 17.
- I think death is the most wonderful invention of life. It purges the system of these old models that are obsolete. I think that's one of Apple's challenges, really. When two young people walk in with the next thing, are we going to embrace it and say this is fantastic? Are we going to be willing to drop our models, or are we going to explain it away? I think we'll do better, because we're completely aware of it and we make it a priority.
- I think the things you most regret in life are things you didn't do. What you really regret was never asking that girl

to dance. In business, if I knew earlier what I know now, I'd have probably done some things a lot better than I did, but I also would've probably done some other things a lot worse. But so what? It's more important to be engaged in the present.

- Life has become very easy with these technologies. We can reach to those people which were not possible before. These things affect life a lot. I do not consider this thing less important.
- My life is simple and easy. I have got a family – Apple and Picture. I don't need anything else.
- Sometimes life is going to hit you in the head with a brick. Don't lose faith. I'm convinced that the only thing that kept me going was that I loved what I did.
- There are different things in life you can do. You can become a painter, you can become a sculptor. You can make something by yourself. But that's not what I do. I do the other thing, which is, you work at things that one person can't do, and that you need large numbers of people to do. I know people like symbols, but it's always unsettling when people write stories about me, because they tend to overlook a lot of other people.
- Your life is limited and hence do not waste it living others life, do not get trapped in wasteful thinking's. Do not move your life according to others. In the noise of others thinking's do not let your inner voice and your intuitions die. They from start know what do you want to become and rest all are subsidiary.

Love

- I love it when you can bring really great design and simple capability to something that doesn't cost much. It was the original vision for Apple. That's what we tried to do with the first Mac. That's what we did with the iPod.

- The only way to do great work is to love what you do. If you haven't found it yet, keep looking. Don't settle. As with all matters of the heart, you'll know when you find it.

Lucky

- I can tell you this: I've been married for 8 years, and that's had a really good influence on me. I've been very lucky, through random happenstance I just happened to sit next to this wonderful woman who became my wife. And it was a big deal. We have 3 kids, and it's been a big deal. You see the world differently.

❑

Mac

- I don't think I've ever worked so hard on something, but working on Macintosh was the neatest experience of my life. Almost everyone who worked on it will say that. None of us wanted to release it at the end. It was as though we knew that once it was out of our hands, it wouldn't be ours anymore. When we finally presented it at the shareholders' meeting, everyone in the auditorium gave it a five-minute ovation. What was incredible to me was that I could see the Mac team in the first few rows. It was as though none of us could believe we'd actually finished it. Everyone started crying.
- I want to tell you my opinion about Microsoft. In the past 10 years they had only two aims, i.e. firstly to copy Mac and secondly to copy Lotus in computer location. And in these 10 years they had fulfilled both their aims and now they can't understand what to do ahead. It was easy to copy Mac because in 10 years there have been no changes in it. It is surprising that Microsoft took then years to copy Mac.

Macintosh

- I do not think that I have worked so hard for anything, but for Macintosh was my life's the biggest experience. All the people who had worked for it would say the same as me. In the end no one among us wanted this to come in the market because we were feeling that once it goes out of our hands in the market then it would never be ours anymore.

- Part of what made the Macintosh great was that the people working on it were musicians, poets, and artists, and zoologists, and historians. They also happened to be the best computer scientists in the world. But if it hadn't been computer science, these people would have been doing amazing things in other fields.
- The Macintosh was sort of like this wonderful romance in your life that you once had—and that produced about 10 million children. In a way it will never be over in your life. You'll still smell that romance every morning when you get up. And when you open the window, the cool air will hit your face, and you'll smell that romance in the air. And you'll see your children around, and you feel good about it. And nothing will ever make you feel bad about it.
- The way you love someone in life is how Macintosh was created and it gave birth to one crore children. This is not going to stop, today also your attachment with it you can feel in your heart every morning.

Man

- Being the richest man in the cemetery doesn't matter to me. Going to bed at night saying we've done something wonderful, that's what matters to me.

Mantras

- This one is from some of my mantras, 'Centered attention and Simplicity.' Simple things can also become difficult than complex things – we have to work hard for making our thinking simple and clean. In the end this hard work is achieved because once you have achieved this then you can even shake the mountains.

Market

- And it comes from saying no to 1,000 things to make sure we don't get on the wrong track or try to do too much. We're always thinking about new markets we could enter, but it's only by saying no that you can concentrate on the things that are really important.
- It comes from saying no to 1,000 things to make sure we don't get on the wrong track or try to do too much. We're always thinking about new markets we could enter, but it's only by saying no that you can concentrate on the things that are really important.

Microsoft

- I am saddened, not by Microsoft's success — I have no problem with their success. They've earned their success, for the most part. I have a problem with the fact that they just make really third-rate products.
- If I were running Apple, I would milk the Macintosh for all it's worth—and get busy on the next great thing. The PC wars are over. Microsoft won a long time ago.
- It wasn't that Microsoft was so brilliant or clever in copying the Mac, it's that the Mac was a sitting duck for 10 years. That's Apple's problem: Their differentiation evaporated.
- Microsoft shamelessly is going on imitating us. But the fact is that our products would come in the market in the end of Tiger month and whereas its products would take still two years to enter the market.

- Our friends up north at Microsoft spend over five billion dollars on research and development and all they seem to do is copy Google and Apple.
- The only problem with Microsoft is that they just have no taste. They have absolutely no taste, and I don't mean that in a small way, I mean that in a big way. They don't think of original ideas and they don't bring much culture into their product. You say why is that important? Proportionally spaced fonts come from type-setting and beautiful books that are where one gets the idea. If it weren't for the Mac, they would never have that in their products. So I'm saddened—not by Microsoft's success, I have no problem with their success. They've earned their success, for the most part. I have a problem with the fact that they just make really third-rate products. Their products have no spirit to them. They have no spirit of enlightenment about them. They are very pedestrian. And the sad part is that a lot of customers don't have a lot of that spirit either. But the way we're going to ratchet up our species is to take the best and spread it around everybody so that everybody grows up with better things and starts to understand the subtlety of these better things. And Microsoft's just McDonald's.
- Unfortunately, people are not rebelling against Microsoft. They don't know any better.
- Why do I call Microsoft as IBM of 90's? This is a company in which the people don't think much about the product because they buy readymade products. It has such an impact on the market that due it the industry is being badly affected. I don't want to argue if Microsoft is capable or not because other people might be doing this. I am just seeing it as a viewer and I am thinking it to be against the benefit of the country.

Mind

- Always keep one thing in mind that we have started with a new ideal and whatever we will do; we will always take care of good quality and would not do any kind of mistake.

Mirror

- For the past 33 years, I have looked in the mirror every morning and asked myself: 'If today were the last day of my life, would I want to do what I am about to do today?' And whenever the answer has been 'No' for too many days in a row, I know I need to change something.

Mistakes

- Sometimes when you innovate, you make mistakes. It is best to admit them quickly, and get on with improving your other innovations.
- When you do inventions then you also commit mistakes and hence it is always better to accept your mistakes instantly and thereafter improve our mistakes of inventions.

Model

- My model for business is the Beatles. They were four guys who kept each other's kind of negative tendencies in check. They balanced each other, and the total was greater than the sum of the parts. That's how I see business: Great things in business are never done by one person, they're done by a team of people.

Moment

- That's the moment that an artist really decides who he or she is. If they keep on risking failure, they're still artists. Dylan and Picasso were always risking failure. This Apple thing is that way for me. I don't want to fail, of course. But even though I didn't know how bad things really were, I still had a lot to think about before I said yes. I had to consider the implications for Pixar, for my family, for my reputation. I decided that I didn't really care, because this is what I want to do. If I try my best and fail, well, I tried my best. What makes you become conservative is realizing that you have something to lose.

Money

- Even if we lose our money, we'll have a company. For once in our lives, we'll have a company.
- I was worth about over a million dollars when I was twenty-three and over ten million dollars when I was twenty-four, and over a hundred million dollars when I was twenty-five and it wasn't that important because I never did it for the money.

Monopoly

- How is the end of monopoly done? Think and see. There are only few handful people who are manufacturing better quality products and the company maintains it. But the people attached with the products do not take the company ahead. This is the work of people attached with marketing who make the business reach worldwide.

Mother

- My biological mother later found out that my mother had never graduated from college and that my father had never graduated from high school. She refused to sign the final adoption papers. She only relented a few months later when my parents promised that I would someday go to college.

Motivations

- The older I get, the more I see how much motivations matter. The Zune was crappy because the people at Microsoft don't really love music or art the way we do. We won because we personally love music.

Mouse

- First was the mouse. The second was the click wheel. And now, we're going to bring multi-touch to the market. And each of these revolutionary interfaces has made possible a revolutionary product-the Mac, the iPod and now the iPhone.

Music

- I'm going to put music in your pocket.
- Music is good for the soul.
- The subscription model of buying music is bankrupt. I think you could make available the Second Coming in a subscription model and it might not be successful.

Mystery

- I think different religions are different doors to the same house. Sometimes I think the house exists, and sometimes I don't. It's the great mystery.

❑

Nature

➢ I used to be way over on the nurture side, but I've swung way over to the nature side. And it's because of my sister Mona and having kids. My daughter is 14 months old, and it's already pretty clear what her personality is.

Needle

➢ We will not use any needle. We will use the world's best pointing device. We will be using such indicating devices that we all have been born with them, not only with one but with ten such pointers we have been born. We are going to use our fingers and are going to touch them with our fingers. We have also invented one new technique named 'Multi-touch, ' it is wonderful and it works like a magic.

Network

➢ The most compelling reason for most people to buy a computer for the home will be to link it into a nationwide communications network. We're just in the beginning stages of what will be a truly remarkable breakthrough for most people—as remarkable as the telephone.

Networks

- When you're young, you look at television and think, there's a conspiracy. The networks have conspired to dumb us down. But when you get a little older, you realize that's not true. The networks are in business to give people exactly what they want. That's a far more depressing thought. Conspiracy is optimistic! You can shoot the bastards! We can have a revolution! But the networks are really in business to give people what they want. It's the truth.

NeXT

- The culture that is there in NeXT is that there independent thinking is given importance and generally between us non – acceptance takes place. This happens at every level. A new person does not take mush time to understand that anyone can place his non – acceptance in front of me without any hesitation. This doesn't mean that I can't disagree with them rather it means that the best thought always wins. It is not necessary to see whose idea it was but is it essential to give the best.
- We took three years to make 'NeXT' computers if we give the customers the computer that they want then we make that computer, which they get from us within a year by just talking to us which can keep them happy. On seeing the beginning of this internet, it is very difficult to know that whether they are taking interest in making the companies or just want to make money. I can at least let you know that if they are not scaly interested in making company then they would not be able to lasts for long. This means that if there is no spirit in you then positively you would leave accepting your defeat.

Number

- For this one simple thinking direction is required who tells to go and get the member. Then add the number 2, write the sum there and think that is that sum bigger than the second number. Imagine 10,00,000 per second, 1, 10, and 00, 000 per second. We get the solution which seems like a magic to us.

❑

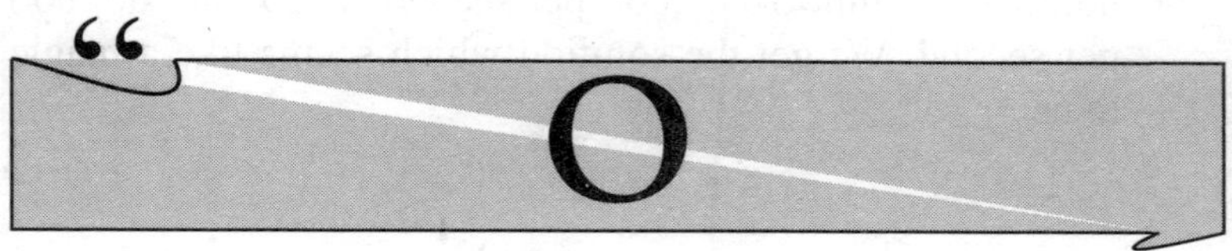

Observation

➢ My observation, is that the doers are the major thinkers. The people that really create the things that change this industry are both the thinker and doer in one person. And if we really go back and we examine, you know, did Leonardo have a guy off to the side that was thinking five years out in the future what he would paint or the technology he would use to paint it, of course not. Leonardo was the artist but he also mixed all his own paints. He also was a fairly good chemist. He knew about pigments, knew about human anatomy. And combining all of those skills together, the art and the science, the thinking and the doing, was what resulted in the exceptional result. And there is no difference in our industry. The people that have really made the contributions have been the thinkers and the doers. And a lot of people of course—it's very easy to take credit for the thinking. The doing is more concrete. But somebody, it's very easy to say, "Oh, I thought of these three years ago." But usually when you dig a little deeper, you find that the people that really did it were also the people that really worked through the hard intellectual problems as well.

Opportunities

- Now when we see new things or opportunities, we can seize them. A creative period like this lasts only maybe a decade, but it can be a golden decade if we manage it properly.
- We do not get the opportunities of doing several jobs and nor can we do all the works best of all because this is only the play of life. Life is short as after some time death appears. We choose this only as the aim of life or else we would have been sitting in Japan's some Buddha temple becoming monks.

Opportunity

- While there's an opportunity to apply software to the living room, the merging of the computer and the TV isn't going to happen. They're really different things. So yes, you want to share some information between the two, but people who are planning to put computers into the living room, like they are today, I'm not sure they're going to have a big success.

Orchestra

- Musicians play their instruments. I play the orchestra.

❑

Passion

- Never let a passion for the perfect take precedence over pragmatism.

PC

- I think back to Detroit in the seventies, when cars were so bad. Why? The people running the companies then didn't love cars. One of the things wrong with the PC industry today is that most of the people running the companies don't love PCs. Does Steve Ballmer love PCs? Does Craig Barrett love PCs? Does Michael Dell love PCs? If Michael Dell wasn't selling PCs he'd be selling something else. These people don't love what they create. And people here do.
- Among the PC companies apple is the creative company, on the other hand Pixar is an entirely entertainment company. Apple brings out new products in the market after a gap of few months. Officials of Apple daily take ten important decisions whereas Pixar releases only one film in a year and as a CEO of this company I just take 3 important decisions in a year and to change them it's very difficult.

People

- As individuals, people are inherently good. I have a somewhat more pessimistic view of people in groups. And I remain extremely concerned when I see what's happening in our country, which is in many ways the luckiest place in the world. We don't seem to be excited about making our country a better place for our kids.
- At the age of 30 to 40 years there are hardly few people who can make wonderful products.
- Don't be trapped by dogma – which is living with the results of other people's thinking. Don't let the noise of others' opinions drown out your own inner voice.
- Few people are saying that to increase the sale of the products America's want to keep on every desk IBM PC with this nothing is going to change. This time to study the user's diversion is a difficult work. Most well known word processing program is of WordStar and it is a manual program of 400 pages. It seems like for writing a novel you will have to read a novel which is like a mystery novel for a common man. This way people would not be able to understand anything and hence to overcome this problem Macintosh was manufactured.
- Hollywood's really different than Silicon Valley. And neither understands the other at all. People up here think being creative is some guys in their late 20s and early 30s sitting around old couches drinking beer thinking up jokes. It couldn't be further from the truth. The creative process is just as disciplined as the technical process; it requires just as much talent. And yet people in Hollywood think technology is only as deep as something you buy. There's no technical culture in Hollywood, they couldn't attract and retain good engineers to save their life, because they're second class

citizens down there. Just like creative people are second class citizens in Silicon Valley.

- I always thought of myself as a humanities person as a kid, but I liked electronics. Then I read something that one of my heroes, Edwin Land of Polaroid, said about the importance of people who could stand at the intersection of humanities and sciences, and I decided that's what I wanted to do.
- I don't think I run roughshod over people, but if something sucks, I tell people to their face. It's my job to be honest. I know what I'm talking about, and I usually turn out to be right. That's the culture I tried to create. We are brutally honest with each other, and anyone can tell me they think I am full of shit and I can tell them the same. And we've had some rip-roaring arguments, where we are yelling at each other, and it's some of the best times I've ever had. I feel totally comfortable saying, "Ron, that store looks like shit" in front of everyone else. Or I might say, God, we really fucked up the engineering on this in front of the person that's responsible. That's the ante for being in the room: You've got to be able to be super honest. Maybe there's a better way, a gentlemen's club where we all wear ties and speak in this Brahmin language and velvet code-words, but I don't know that way, because I am middle class from California.
- I don't want people to dislike me. I'm indifferent to whether they dislike me.
- I found that there were these incredibly great people at doing certain things, and that you couldn't replace one of these people with 50 average people. They could just do things that no number of average people could do.
- I think most creative people want to express appreciation for being able to take advantage of the work that's been done by others before us. I didn't invent the language or mathematics I use. I make little of my own food, none of my

own clothes. Everything I do depends on other members of our species and the shoulders that we stand on. And a lot of us want to contribute something back to our species and to add something to the flow.

- It is not apt to call the people of Silicon Valley, crazy. In the 60s they were called so and in the 70s also there were such people. But people in today's time are not such. Today's people are such that if they would have been in the 60s they would have become poets. They instead of considering computer as a language would look upon it as an entertainment source. They don't look upon it as a mathematician and a society's well wisher.
- It probably is true that the people who have been able to come up with the innovations in many industries are maybe not the people that either are best skilled at, or, frankly enjoy running a large enterprise where they lose contact with the day-to-day workings of that innovative process. Dr. Land at Polaroid, he's a perfect example.
- It's not about pop culture, and it's not about fooling people, and it's not about convincing people that they want something they don't. We figure out what we want. And I think we're pretty good at having the right discipline to think through whether a lot of other people are going to want it, too.
- People get stuck as they get older. Our minds are sort of electrochemical computers. Your thoughts construct patterns like scaffolding in your mind. You are really etching chemical patterns. In most cases, people get stuck in those patterns, just like grooves in a record, and they never get out of them. It's a rare person who etches grooves that are other than a specific way of looking at things, a specific way of questioning things. It's rare that you see an artist in his 30s or 40s able to really contribute something amazing. Of course, there are some people who are innately curious, forever little kids in their awe of life, but they're rare.

- People who have worked for Macintosh, they only are its real power. My job is only to make opportunities available for them and to keep the rest of the team members away from the working people.
- People who know what they're talking about don't need PowerPoint.
- People would be forced to buy a computer for their house because that would keep them in touch with the national network. We are in the initial stages when the computer's importance would be known.
- A lot of people in our industry haven't had very diverse experiences. So they don't have enough dots to connect, and they end up with very linear solutions without a broad perspective on the problem. The broader one understands of the human experience, the better design we will have.
- A lot of times, people don't know what they want until you show it to them.
- A year back I had taken out some people out of the Apple Company but now as on today it is becoming difficult for me to take out anyone from the job. Though I have to do so towards the responsibility that I am holding as of my post. But when I look upon the point of view of a five year old child. I imagine myself in place of that person and try to understand how it feels when on reaching home I have to tell my wife and children that I have been taken out of my job. In 20 years this can happen with my children too. Till date I have not thought upon this matter that intensely that life is too short and one day we all are going to die is the actual truth of life.
- Actually, making an insanely great product has a lot to do with the process of making the product, how you learn things

and adopt new ideas and throw out old ideas. But, yeah, the people who made Mac are sort of on the edge.

- Almost everything—all external expectations, all pride, all fear of embarrassment or failure—these things just fall away in the face of death, leaving only what is truly important. Remembering that you are going to die is the best way I know to avoid the trap of thinking you have something to lose. You are already naked. There is no reason not to follow your heart.
- It's not about pop culture, and it's not about fooling people, and it's not about convincing people that they want something they don't. We figure out what we want. And I think we're pretty good at having the right discipline to think through whether a lot of other people are going to want it, too. That's what we get paid to do.
- The people who are crazy enough to think they can change the world are the ones who do.
- The people who are doing the work are the moving force behind the Macintosh. My job is to create a space for them, to clear out the rest of the organization and keep it at bay.
- The people who built Silicon Valley were engineers. They learned business, they learned a lot of different things, but they had a real belief that humans, if they worked hard with other creative, smart people, could solve most of humankind's problems. I believe that very much.
- When you get really good people, they know they're really good, and you don't have to baby people's egos so much. And what really matters is the work, and everybody knows that. So, people are being counted on to do specific pieces of the puzzle.

- And the most important thing you can do for someone who's really good and really being counted on is to point out to them when their work isn't good enough.
- With the growing age the roots of the people become firm. Our brain is like a computer and stores our thinking in it. You can call them fertile layers and people remain dependant on these layers only. The way dust gets accumulated on the old records similarly people cannot get free from these layers. There are very few people who try to wipe away the dust and look upon the thing in a different way. You can see very rare artists who could show their skills at the age of thirties to forties. No doubt there are many people who have a curious mind with a child like inquisitiveness but there are many few of this kind.

Perfect

- This is true that a person who invents for different companies cannot be very perfect and Polaroid's Doctors are a good example of this.

Person

- How the opposite person does appear? How would he behave during a problematic situation? Why has he come here? I asked everyone – what have come to do here? With the reply you come to know that the kind of person you are trying to find out he is not. This is only the true test.
- I'm the only person I know that's lost a quarter of a billion dollars in one year. It's very character-building.
- It doesn't take a new person long to see that people feel fine about openly disagreeing with me. That doesn't mean I can't

disagree with them, but it does mean that the best ideas win. Our attitude is that we want the best. Don't get hung up on who owns the idea. Pick the best one, and let's go.

Perspective

- So when these people sell out, even though they get fabulously rich, they're gypping themselves out of one of the potentially most rewarding experiences of their unfolding lives. Without it, they may never know their values or how to keep their newfound wealth in perspective.

Piracy

- It is piracy, not overt online music stores, which is our main competitor.
- This is piracy and not an online music store, who is our main rival.

Pirate

- Why join the navy if you can be a pirate?

Pleasure

- Salary increment gives me pleasure and I have experienced it too but I am more attracted to revolutionary changes and maybe because otherwise changes take place with difficult you have to pas three such phase when people talk of you being unsuccessful.

Poet

- I would have been a poet of half talent but coincidentally I have landed up in this field.
- I'm just a guy who probably should have been a semi-talented poet on the Left Bank. I sort of got sidetracked here.

Pointing

- Pointing is a metaphor we all know. We've done a lot of studies and tests on that, and it's much faster to do all kinds of functions, such as cutting and pasting, with a mouse, so it's not only easier to use but more efficient.

Principle

- Our whole company, our whole philosophical base, is founded on one principle. That principle is that there is something very special and very historically different that takes place when you have one computer and one person. Very different than if you have ten people and one computer.

Problem

- The problem is I'm older now, I'm 40 years old, and this stuff doesn't change the world. It really doesn't.
- The problem with the Internet startup craze isn't that too many people are starting companies; it's that too many people aren't sticking with it. That's somewhat understandable, because there are many moments that are filled with despair and agony, when you have to fire people and cancel things and deal with very difficult situations. That's when you find out who you are and what your values are.

Product

- As you might know that my life has always been simple. There had been a flow in my life always with whose support I have been able to move ahead. My belief is that everything begins with an invention of a great product. Hence, for this I believe in listening to the views of the customers. But they cannot tell you that there is going to be a blast in the market which would change the image of the whole market. Hence, will have to listen to the customers attentively but later it's me who have to do the survey and will have to speak and discuss with such people who know about the customer's comfort ability and also imagine the blast. This is only my way of seeing that every beginning is with a great product. I have been lately accused of not taking care of my customers and I accept that to some extent they do hold some weight age.

- For manufacturing a good product many aspects are attached to it like how do you learn and how do you leave old thinking and accept the new one? People who had made Mac had almost passed through this phase.
- I think the same philosophy that drives the product has to drive everything else if you want to have a great company. Manufacturing, for example. Demands just as much thought and strategy as the product. If you don't pay attention to your manufacturing, it will limit the kind of product you can build and engineer. Some companies view manufacturing as a necessary evil, and some view it as something more neutral. But we view it instead as a tremendous opportunity to gain a competitive advantage. I've thought that ever since I visited Japan in the early 80s. And let me add that the same is true of sales and marketing. You need a sales and marketing organization that is oriented toward educating customers rather than just taking orders, providing a real service rather than moving boxes. This is extremely important.
- I think we're having fun. I think our customers really like our products. And we're always trying to do better.
- It is we ourselves who can make our product unique.
- Many companies have decided to segregate, may be this would be best for them. We have chosen a different path. We

believe that if we keep best products in front of the customer then he will positively open his purse to take it.

- Many people make excellent product but due to their companies being weak they don't achieve the goals that should have. In this regard, Hewlett-Packard had been an ideal company. The major achievements had been that they had established a company in real context. No one today remembers that their first product was a frequency encounter. This company sells so many products that its name cannot be associated with any one product. He had established the company and followed these principles for 30 to 40 years. Hence, they could set an example. The principle adopted by Hewlett-Packard was the same as that of the Silicon Valley people.
- Our aim is to make world's best product and not world's largest product.
- The products suck! There's no sex in them anymore!
- There are many such examples when a wonderful product cannot be successful. Windows can be considered as an example in this. But there are such examples also where excellent products have fetched recognition. IPad is an important example in this context.
- We do not say anything about future products. We work on them in secret, then we announce them.
- What we want to do is make a leapfrog product that is way smarter than any mobile device has ever been, and super-easy to use. This is what iPhone is. OK? So, we're going to reinvent the phone.
- I feel that we are enjoying. I feel that our customers in reality like our products and we would always try to improve them.
- I wish developing great products was as easy as writing a check. If that was the case, Microsoft would have great products.

- If anybody's going to make our products obsolete, I want it to be us.
- If I look at myself and ask, 'What am I best at and what do I enjoy most doing?' I think what I'm best at is creating sort of new innovative products.
- It is difficult to prepare designs of the products by focusing only on a group. Until you do not tell people then they do not understand what they have to do.

Profit

- If you keep your eye on the profit, you're going to skimp on the product. But if you focus on making really great products, then the profits will follow.

Proud

- I'm as proud of many of the things we haven't done as the things we have done. Innovation is saying no to a thousand things.
- I'm as proud of many of the things we haven't done as the things we have done. Innovation is saying no to a thousand things.

Provoke

- This is not a talk of any pop culture and nor is it of making fool of anyone. We also don't want to provoke anyone to buy any such product which they are not in need of. In fact we try to find out what we want. When we feel that some product would be beneficial for us then we reach to a conclusion that the same product would be useful for others too. This way we have been achieving success. We cannot go outside and ask people what would be the great product of future. In this context we can say Henry Ford's words, "If I would had asked my customers what they want then am sure they would had demanded from me a very fast riding horse."

Purpose

➢ The only purpose for me in building a company is so that it can make products. Of course, building a very strong company and a foundation of talent and culture is essential over the long run to keep making great products. On the other hand, to me, the company is one of humanity's most amazing inventions. It's totally abstract. Sure, you have to build something with bricks and mortar to put the people in, but basically a company is this abstract construct we've invented, and it's incredibly powerful.

Pushing

➢ You always have to keep pushing to innovate. Dylan could have sung protest songs forever and probably made a lot of money, but he didn't. He had to move on, and when he did, by going electric in 1965, he alienated a lot of people. His 1966 Europe tour was his greatest. The Beatles were the same way. They kept evolving, moving, and refining their art. That's what I've always tried to do—keep moving. Otherwise, as Dylan says, if you are not busy being born, you're busy dying.

❑

Qualifications

- When I appoint any senior person than it is basically depended on his qualifications. It is important for them to be smart. But the most important question is that will they keep deep attachment with Apple. If they fell in love with Apple then everything will easily happen on its own. Then only they will work for the benefit of Apple continuously. Then they will stop thinking of their own benefit, Steve's benefit or for that matter anyone else's benefit.

Qualitative

- Make yourself a scale of qualitative. Some people are not habituate of this surrounding where excellence is criticized.

Quality

- Be a yardstick of quality. Some people aren't used to an environment where excellence is expected.
- Be the scale of measuring quality. Many people are not able to adjust where there are expectations of excellence.
- Be the symbol of quality. Some people are not habituate of the surrounding where excellence is expected.

- Quality is more important than quantity. One home run is much better than two doubles.

Quote

- Here's to the crazy ones—the misfits, the rebels, the troublemakers, the round pegs in the square holes. The ones who see things differently—they're not fond of rules. You can quote them, disagree with them, glorify or vilify them, but the only thing you can't do is ignore them because they change things. They push the human race forward, and while some may see them as the crazy ones, we see genius, because the ones, who are crazy enough to think that they can change the world, are the ones who do.
- There's an old Wayne Gretzky quote that I love. 'I skate to where the puck is going to be, not where it has been.' And we've always tried to do that at Apple. Since the very beginning. And we always will.
- When I was 17, I read a quote that went something like: "If you live each day as if it was your last, someday you'll most certainly be right." It made an impression on me, and since then, for the past 33 years, I have looked in the mirror every morning and asked myself: "If today were the last day of my life, would I want to do what I am about to do today?" And whenever the answer has been "no" for too many days in a row, I know I need to change something.

❑

Reason

- The reason I went back to Apple is that I feel like the world would be a better place with Apple in it than not. And it's hard to imagine the world without Apple now.
- The reason that Apple is able to create products like the iPad is because we've always tried to be at the intersection of technology and the liberal arts.
- The reason we wouldn't make a seven-inch tablet isn't because we don't want to hit a price point, it's because we don't think you can make a great tablet with a seven-inch screen.

Recruiting

- Recruiting is hard. It's just finding the needles in the haystack. We do it ourselves and we spend a lot of time at it. I've participated in the hiring of maybe 5, 000-plus people in my life. So I take it very seriously. You can't know enough in a one-hour interview. So, in the end, it's ultimately based on your gut. How do I feel about this person? What are they like when they're challenged? Why are they here? I ask everybody that: "Why are you here?" The answers themselves are not what you're looking for. It's the meta-data.

Reinvent

- We want to reinvent the phone. What's the killer app? The killer app is making calls! It's amazing how hard it is to make calls on most phones. We want to let you use contacts like never before-sync your iPhone with your PC or Mac.

Relation

- If you have not got this then you keep on searching it, don't accept your defeat. As it happens with all the things of our heart, if you get it then you will yourself understand it and also similarly to any memorable relation who with the span of times it becomes better and stronger.

Remember

- One way to remember who you are is to remember who your heroes are.

Remembering

- Remembering that I'll be dead soon is the most important tool I've ever encountered to help me make the big choices in life. Because almost everything—all external expectations, all pride, all fear of embarrassment or failure—these things just fall away in the face of death, leaving only what is truly important. Remembering that you are going to die is the best way I know to avoid the trap of thinking you have something to lose. You are already naked. There is no reason not to follow your heart.
- Remembering that you are going to die is the best way I know to avoid the trap of thinking you have something to

lose. You are already naked. There is no reason not to follow your heart.

Replaced

- The heaviness of being successful was replaced by the lightness of being a beginner again—less sure about everything. It freed me to enter one of the most creative periods of my life.

Research

- We do not do any sort of market research and nor do we hire any consultancy services. In the period of ten years only once I have taken consultancy services of a consultant at that time when I wanted to do analyses for the retail market for Gateway. Because Apple while opening retail stores did not wanted the same mistakes that it had committed during launching of Gateway. After this till date we have never taken any services of the consultants as we believe in making the entire product on our own.

Resource

- My favorite things in life don't cost any money. It's really clear that the most precious resource we all have is time.

Respect

- I have a great respect for incremental improvement, and I've done that sort of thing in my life, but I've always been attracted to the more revolutionary changes. I don't know why. Because they're harder. They're much more stressful emotionally. And you usually go through a period where everybody tells you that you've completely failed.

➢ If they are working in an environment where excellence is expected, then they will do excellent work without anything but self-motivation. I'm talking about an environment in which excellence is noticed and respected and is in the culture. If you have that, you don't have to tell people to do excellent work. They understand it from their surroundings.

Responsibility

➢ To have wealth more than you can spend in your life time is a big responsibility. I feel I should spend away my all wealth till I am alive. You cannot go away leaving lots of wealth behind you. Such wealth can finish off your children. If you die without kids then your entire wealth will go to the government. Everyone thinks that in place of government they can use the money in better way for the welfare of the people. It is a challenge that how could we spent our wealth when we are alive and how should it also be returned to the society.

Responsible

➢ The team should be easy and clear and at the same time should be responsible too. This way all work becomes easier. Unity and simplicity are the two major points. Initially you will have to work hard for presenting your opinions in a simple manner but when once you have done so then you can make impossible to possible.

Result

➢ This is not an issue of wonders or status, rather it is a matter of results and products and it is the matter of those past things for which people working in Apple and people working outside. Apple is getting enthusiastic of this company because they understand what Apple is and what its capacity of contribution in the industry is.

- It takes these very simple-minded instructions—'Go fetch a number, add it to this number, put the result there, perceive if it's greater than this other number'—but executes them at a rate of, let's say, 10,00,000 per second. At 10,00,000 per second, the results appear to be magic.

Revolution

- The things that are yet to be developed by the computer or its software with that we are going to bring a revolution change in our learning style.
- This is a revolution, an information revolution and so does it is also a free energy revolution. Its appearance is – free mental energy. It sounds very odd but it is true as our Macintosh had been working at an electricity unit less than the units used in 100 watts bulb. With this you can save electricity of several hours. This way we are giving to the people what they want.
- This revolution, the information revolution, is a revolution of free energy as well, but of another kind: free intellectual energy. It's very crude today, yet our Macintosh computer takes less power than a 100-watt bulb to run it and it can save you hours a day. What will it be able to do ten or twenty years from now, or fifty years from now?

Rewarding

- The rewarding thing isn't merely to start a company or to take it public. It's like when you're a parent. Although the birth experience is a miracle, what's truly rewarding is living with your child and helping him grow up.

❑

School

- My mother taught me to read before I went to school, so I was pretty bored in school, and I turned into a little terror. You should have seen us in third grade. We basically destroyed our teacher. We would let snakes loose in the classroom and explode bombs. Things changed in the fourth grade, though. One of the saints in my life is this woman named Imogene Hill, who was a fourth-grade teacher who taught this advanced class. She got hip to my whole situation in about a month and kindled a passion in me for learning things. I learned more that year than I think I learned in any year in school.

Science

- I learned about serif and san serif typefaces, about varying the amount of space between different letter combinations, about what makes great typography great. It was beautiful, historical, artistically subtle in a way that science can't capture, and I found it fascinating.

Sense

- I'm an optimist in the sense that I believe humans are noble and honorable, and some of them are really smart. I have a very optimistic view of individuals. As individuals, people are inherently good. I have a somewhat more pessimistic view of people in groups. And I remain extremely concerned when I see what's happening in our country, which is in many ways the luckiest place in the world. We don't seem to be excited about making our country a better place for our kids.

Settle

- If you haven't found it yet, keep looking. Don't settle. As with all matters of the heart, you'll know when you find it. And like any great relationship, it just gets better and better as the years roll on.
- If you haven't found it yet, keep looking. Don't settle. As with all matters of the heart, you'll know when you find it. And, like any great relationship, it just gets better and better as the years roll on.

Shameless

- They are shamelessly trying to copy us. I think the most telling thing is that OS X Tiger will ship at the end of the month and Windows Vista is still two years out. They can't even copy fast.

Silicon

- I don't understand what is this valley? I work in Apple for hours and don't go to other places and so don't know about this Silicon Valley. According to me, it is a group of artists who concentrate only on their art and on nothing else. To search for a lover is important, to cook tasty food is also important, joining of a job in the army is also essential and many other things like them are important. Artists don't pay attention to these routine things. These people are so engrossed in their work that they don't bother about other. Among these many have taken this path after a lot of thinking.

Sit

- If you just sit and observe, you will see how restless your mind is. If you try to calm it, it only makes it worse, but over time it does calm, and when it does, there's room to hear more subtle things—that's when your intuition starts to blossom and you start to see things more clearly and be in the present more. Your mind just slows down, and you see a tremendous expanse in the moment. You see so much more than you could see before. It's a discipline; you have to practice it.

Sleep

- For you to sleep well at night, the aesthetic, the quality, has to be carried all the way through.

Slowly

- Things happen fairly slowly, you know. They do. These waves of technology, you can see them way before they happen, and you just have to choose wisely which ones you're going to surf. If you choose unwisely, then you can waste a lot of energy, but if you choose wisely it actually unfolds fairly slowly. It takes years. One of our biggest insights years ago was that we didn't want to get into any business where we didn't own or control the primary technology because you'll get your head handed to you.

Sofa

- Generally for most of the people literal meaning of design is coloring, interior decorating or color of the sofa and curtains. But for me design does not mean only this. Design is the man made product's soul, through which a person displays his inner beauty, then let it be in the form of a product manufacturing or in the form of a service to mankind. 'Mac' did not meant some special color or shape. The specialty of iMac is that it is made very useful for the customers. It is manufactured on the basis of the computer, in which all the mechanisms meet. The new iPad that we have made; while making it I had decided that it has to be kept away from the fan. Because it would be so satisfying to work with such computer which never makes sound. But this was not possible only with my decision, for it lot of technical support had to be taken. For arranging better electricity we had to shed lots of sweat. This did not keep any relation with colors. The days since we have started manufacturing products our aim has been this only.

Software

- Our personal opinion is that software should also be used in living room too. But merging of computer with television is not good. As both are two separate things. People planning to make the place of computer in living room in my opinion they will not get notable success.
- Software becomes the part of the experience of the customers. IPad and iTunes have proved this. Today Apple's technology also incites other technology products other than computers.

Solution

- When you are trying to find out the answer of some problem then first solution would always be complicated and most of the people would then leave trying. But remember if you continue trying then you would surely get and easier way out. Actually people don't want to waste their energy and time in finding the solutions. We agree that a customer adopts such a product that has been manufactured after a lot of research has been done on it.
- When you first start off trying to solve a problem, the first solutions you come up with are very complex, and most people stop there. But if you keep going, and live with the problem and peel more layers of the onion off, you can often-times arrive at some very elegant and simple solutions. Most people just don't put in the time or energy to get there.

Songs

- A hundred songs. A thousand songs. Five hundred songs. Somewhere between five hundred and a thousand songs. Right in your pocket. Because I can't stand looking at that ridiculous Walkman anymore. You're carrying around a brick playing a cassette tape. We're not savages. I'm going to put a thousand songs in your pocket.
- Now, we are selling over 5 million songs a day now. Isn't that unbelievable? That's 58 songs every second of every minute of every hour of every day.

Sony

- I would rather compete with Sony than compete in another product category with Microsoft. That's because Sony has to rely on other companies to make its software. We're the only company that owns the whole widget—the hardware, the software, and the operating system. We can take full responsibility for the user experience. We can do things that the other guy can't do.

Sorry

- I'm sorry, it's true. Having children really changes your view on these things. We're born, we live for a brief instant, and we die. It's been happening for a long time. Technology is not changing it much—if at all.

Soul

- Dr. Edwin Land was a name of a restless soul who left his studies in between in Harvard and then established Polaroid. He was a great inventor of our time and after understanding the depth of art and science he established a strong team. Polaroid had adopted his thinking for several years. But great inventor Dr. Land was asked to leave his own institution. Such an odd thing I had never heard before. We can call him a national hero but don't know why people couldn't accept him as an ideal hero. To become Dr. Land is important than becoming an astronaut and a football player.

Special

- Knowing I was adopted may have made me feel more independent, but I have never felt abandoned. I've always felt special. My parents made me feel special.

Stay

- Stay hungry. Stay foolish.

Study

- I read a study that measured the efficiency of locomotion for various species on the planet. The condor used the least energy to move a kilometer. Humans came in with a rather unimpressive showing about a third of the way down the list. That didn't look so good, but then someone at Scientific American had the insight to test the efficiency of lomotion for a man on a bicycle and a man on a bicycle blew the condor away.

Styles

- Who wants styles (needles)? You need take them out, keep them aside and then get lost. No one needs styles.

Stylus

- So let's not use a stylus. We're going to use the best pointing device in the world. We're going to use a pointing device that we're all born with-born with ten of them. We're going to use our fingers. We're going to touch this with our fingers. And we have invented a new technology called multi-touch, which is phenomenal. It works like magic.

Success

- Even though some people have come out with neat products, if their company is perceived as a sweatshop or a revolving door, it's not considered much of a success. Remember, the role models were Hewlett and Packard. Their main achievement was that they built a company. Nobody remembers their first frequency counter, their first audio oscillator, their first this or that. And they sell so many products now that no one person really symbolizes the company…And they built a company and they lived that philosophy for 35 or 40 years and that's why they're heroes. Hewlett and Packard started what became the Silicon Valley.

- I don't really care about being right, I just care about success. You'll find a lot of people that will tell you I had a very strong opinion, and they presented evidence to the contrary and five minutes later I changed my mind. I don't mind being wrong, and I'll admit that I'm wrong a lot. It doesn't really matter to me too much. What matters to me is that we do the right thing.
- I'm convinced that about half of what separates the successful entrepreneurs from the non-successful ones is pure perseverance.
- If you really look closely, most overnight successes took a long time.
- If you want to establish a successful company then you would have to use the same thinking that you had used while making the product. For example, I want to write an account of the product and for that the same thinking is required that was needed to make the product. Some companies dislike the product while others show their liking towards it but we look upon this as an opportunity through which the advantages of competitions can be achieved. After travelling to Japan in 80s later on my opinion has been this. In this manner for marketing and sales also a strong strategy is required. You should have such a team for them that they can instead of taking orders from the customers they would spread awareness among them.
- I'm as proud of what we don't do as I am of what we do.

- I'm convinced that about half of what separates the successful entrepreneurs from the non-successful ones is pure perseverance.

Swallow

- Nobody has tried to swallow us since I've been here. I think they are afraid how we would taste.

System

- The system is that there is no system. That doesn't mean we don't have process. Apple is a very disciplined company, and we have great processes. But that's not what it's about. Process makes you more efficient.

❑

Tablet

- We will not make 7 inch tablet because we do not want to fight at lower prices. Whereas we also understand that a very good tablet cannot be made with just a 7 inch screen.

Tablets

- The seven inch tablets are tweeners: too big to compete with a smartphone, and too small to compete with an iPad.

Technique

- It is in all not that necessary that a new technique cannot replace the old technique but for sure it would bring changes and in the form of new changes and that also as a new definition and thereby slowly in the end it would change it. It would be in the same manner as some people did not replace their black and white TV till they got colored TV.

Techniques

- We all are aware of the sign techniques. We have not done any study or efforts on these products. Several kinds of jobs become easy to do with them like cut and paste that also with the help of the mouse. It is not only easy in use but also very useful.

Technologies

- The technologies can make life easier; can let us touch people we might not otherwise. You may have a child with a birth defect and be able to get in touch with other parents and support groups, get medical information, the latest experimental drugs. These things can profoundly influence life. I'm not downplaying that.

Technology

- The overall point is that new technology will not necessarily replace old technology, but it will date it. By definition. Eventually, it will replace it. But it's like people who had black-and-white TVs when color came out. They eventually decided whether or not the new technology was worth the investment.
- I've always wanted to own and control the primary technology in everything we do.
- In everything it takes time and you also know that. Before the incarnation of technological waves we can presume it. Then you have to choose it with intelligence that in which direction you have to work. If yòu do a mistake in choosing then your energy would go waste. But if you choose with intelligence then it would be a slow process. It may take many years too. Years back we had decided that we would never produce such products whose basic technology would not be in our hands; this was ours perfect decision. Because on doing so you have to depend on others.
- It is unfortunate but yet true that one's way of seeing changes if their children is there in that place. We take birth and are alive while and after that we die. This is being carried on

since very long. Technology could not have been succeeded in this pattern at all.

- I've always wanted to own and control the primary technology in everything we do.
- I've done a lot of things I'm not proud of, such as getting my girlfriend pregnant when I was 23 and the way I handled that.
- Technology is nothing. What's important is that you have a faith in people, that they're basically good and smart, and if you give them tools, they'll do wonderful things with them.
- The technology crashed and burned at Xerox. Why? I learned more about this with John Sculley later on. What happens is, John came from PepsiCo.. And they—at most—would change their product once every 10 years. To them, a new product was a new sized bottle. So if you were a "product person, " you couldn't change the course of that company very much. So, who influences the success at PepsiCo.? The sales and marketing people. Therefore they were the ones that got promoted, and they were the ones that ran the company. Well, for PepsiCo. that might have been okay, but it turns out the same thing can happen at technology companies that get monopolies. Like IBM and Xerox. If you are a "product person" at IBM or Xerox, you make a better copier or better computer. So what? When you have a monopoly market-share, the company's not any more successful. So the people who make the company more successful are the sales and marketing people, and they end up running the companies. And the "product people" get run out of the decision-making forums. The companies forget how to make great products. The product sensibility and product genius that brought them to this monopolistic position gets rotted out by people running these companies who have no conception of a good product versus a bad product. They have no conception of the craftsmanship that's required to take a good idea and

turn it into a good product. And they really have no feeling in their hearts about wanting to help the customers.

- With our technology, with objects, literally three people in a garage can blow away what 200 people at Microsoft can do. Literally can blow it away. Corporate America has a need that is so huge and can save them so much money, or make them so much money, or cost them so much money if they miss it, that they are going to fuel the object revolution.

Temptation

- There is a temptation in our networked age to think that ideas can be developed by email and iChat. That is crazy. Creativity comes from spontaneous meetings, from random discussions. You run into someone, you ask what they are doing, you say, 'Wow' and soon you are cooking up all sorts of ideas.

Thing

- If you ask someone who makes a new thing that how did he do this then he would feel little guilty, because he himself had not made it, he had just seen this way somewhere. After some time they start feeling this as normal. This happens because now they can join their experiences these by transforming them into new things.

Things

- But it's a disservice to constantly put things in this radical new light—that it's going to change everything. Things don't have to change the world to be important.
- Ultimately, it comes down to taste. It comes down to trying to expose yourself to the best things that humans have done

and then try to bring those things into what you're doing. Picasso had a saying: good artists copy, great artists steal. And we have always been shameless about stealing great ideas, and I think part of what made the Macintosh great was that the people working on it were musicians and poets and artists and zoologists and historians who also happened to be the best computer scientists in the world.

- We do not get lost or do not get entangled in other things and hence we have to leave away many things. We always keep on thinking for entering into new markets and in doing so instead of paying attention towards non important things we only focus towards important things.
- We don't get a chance to do that many things, and everyone should be really excellent. Because this is our life. Life is brief, and then you die, you know? So this is what we've chosen to do with our life.
- We have till here saying No-to 1000 things, because we want to be sure that we do not go away on wrong path or we do not land up doing something too much. We always think about the new market where we can get an opportunity to enter only after saying no, you can concentrate on things that are important.
- We hire people who want to make the best things in the world.
- With many things—high-performance automobiles, for example—the aesthetic comes right from the function, and I suppose electronics is no different. But I've also found that the best companies pay attention to aesthetics. They take the extra time to lay out grids and proportion things appropriately, and it seems to pay off for them. I mean, beyond the functional benefits, the aesthetic communicates

something about how they think of themselves, their sense of discipline in engineering, how they run their company, stuff like that.

Think

- I think (calling Silicon Valley workers "nerds" is) an antiquated notion. There were people in the 60s who were like that and even in the early 70s, but now they're not that way. Now they're the people who would have been poets had they lived in the 60s. And they're looking at computers as their medium of expression rather than language, rather than being a mathematician and using mathematics, rather than, you know, writing social theories.
- We think Android is very, very fragmented, and becoming more fragmented by the day. And as you know, Apple strives for the integrated model so that the user isn't forced to be the systems integrator.
- We think basically you watch television to turn your brain off, and you work on your computer when you want to turn your brain on.
- We think the Mac will sell zillions, but we didn't build the Mac for anybody else. We built it for ourselves. We were the group of people who were going to judge whether it was great or not. We weren't going to go out and do market research. We just wanted to build the best thing we could build.
- When we took (the original iMac prototype) to the engineers, they said, "Oh." And they came up with 38 reasons (it couldn't be done). And I said, "No, no, we're doing this."

And they said, "Well, why?" And I said, "Because I'm the CEO, and I think it can be done." And so they kind of begrudgingly did it. But then it was a big hit.

Time

- Your time is limited, so don't waste it living someone else's life. Don't be trapped by dogma—which is living with the results of other people's thinking. Don't let the noise of others' opinions drown out your own inner voice. And most important, have the courage to follow your heart and intuition. They somehow already know what you truly want to become. Everything else is secondary.
- We all are busy and we do not have this much time that we try to understand the proper functioning of the washing machine or phone. If you have one phone then you will never be able to know more than 5 percent qualities of its and nor will you be able to use more than 5 percent of its qualities because you feel it to be a complex work. It is a very strange situation that we all are living a very busy life. We have or jobs, likes and our children, everyone's life is busy, the entire society seems busy. Actually you do not have time to learn the details of the products and you find everything like before.

Tool

- What a computer is to me is the most remarkable tool that we have ever come up with. It's the equivalent of a bicycle for our minds.

Tools

- It's not the tools that you have faith in—tools are just tools. They work, or they don't work. Its people you have faith in or not. I mean, I get pessimistic sometimes, but not for long.

Top Line

➢ Somebody once told me, "Manage the top line, and the bottom line will follow." What's the top line? Its things like, why are we doing this in the first place? What's our strategy? What are customers saying? How responsive are we? Do we have the best products and the best people? Those are the kind of questions you have to focus on.

Track

➢ We've demonstrated a strong track record of being much disciplined with the use of our cash. We don't let it burn a hole in our pocket; we don't allow it to motivate us to do stupid acquisitions. And so I think that we'd like to continue to keep our powder dry, because we do feel that there are one or more strategic opportunities in the future.

Trade

➢ I would trade all of my technology for an afternoon with Socrates.

True

➢ I'm sorry, it's true. Having children really changes your view on these things. We're born, we live for a brief instant, and we die. It's been happening for a long time. Technology is not changing it much – if at all.

❑

Understand

- I understand that it has got the world very closer and so will these distances ahead would reduce further more. Everything has its negative qualities too. Everything's unfavorable result also comes in front. The biggest destroyer of technology is television and television at the same time in its excellence is also a wonderful invention too.
- I understand that this time one war is on which is going between the people producing new products and the customers and at present iPhone and iPad are the winners.
- Most people have no concept of how an automatic transmission works, yet they know how to drive a car. You don't have to study physics to understand the laws of motion to drive a car. You don't have to understand any of this stuff to use Macintosh.

Universe

- I want to put a ding in the universe.

❑

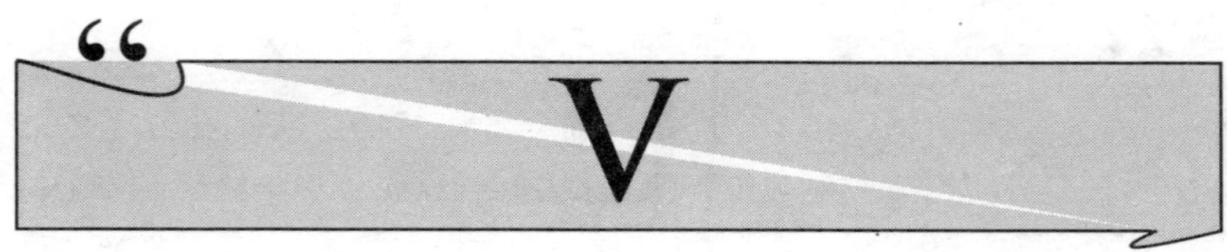

View

- I think really great products come from melding two points of view—the technology point of view and the customer point of view. You need both.

Virgin

- I am a fruitarian and I will only eat leaves picked by virgins in the moonlight. (He was joking. Probably.)

Vision

- If you are working on something exciting that you really care about, you don't have to be pushed. The vision pulls you.
- My vision was to create the first fully packaged computer. We were no longer aiming for the handful of hobbyists who liked to assemble their own computers, who knew how to buy transformers and keyboards. For every one of them there were a thousand people who would want the machine to be ready to run.
- We're gambling on our vision, and we would rather do that than make "me too" products. Let some other companies do that. For us, it's always the next dream.

Volkswagen Bug

- When I was growing up, a guy across the street had a Volkswagen Bug. He really wanted to make it into a Porsche. He spent all his spare money and time accessorizing this VW, making it look and sound loud. By the time he was done, he did not have a Porsche. He had a loud, ugly VW.

❑

Watching

- The experience of watching it happen is quite different from the experience of imagining it happen. I think everybody who had anything to do with creating the Mac has very, very good feelings about it.

Wealth

- When I was 23 years old I had 10 lakh dollars, at the age of 24 years I had one crore dollars and at the age of 25 years I had 10 crore dollars. But wealth had no much importance in my life because I had not worked only for money.

What

- Older people sit down and ask, 'What is it?' but the boy asks, 'What can I do with it?'

Wish

- I wish him the best, I really do. I just think he and Microsoft are a bit narrow. He'd be a broader guy if he had dropped acid once or gone off to an ashram when he was younger.
- I wish that bells ring in the universe.

Wonderful

- We went on the roof top and said, "We have a wonderful thing with us. While making this we have also used your components also. Will you give us some funds for further manufacturing it or we will make it and give you. We are only interested in making it. Keep us on salary we would work for you." They told, "No." Then we went to Hewlett Packard and they said to us, "We don't need you. You have not even finished your college studies."

WordStar

- The manual for WordStar, the most popular word-processing program, is 400 pages thick. To write a novel, you have to read a novel-one that reads like a mystery to most people. They're not going to learn slash q-z any more than they're going to learn Morse code. That is what Macintosh is all about.
- Word star which is the most well known word processing program has a manual of 400 pages. In this regard for writing one novel we need to read the other novel which one on reading it would feel it to be like a mystery. Today people are not going to learn slash Q-Z in the same manner as no one is today interested in learning the Morse code. The usefulness of Macintosh is not visible.

Work

- I look at myself and ask myself, "What work I can do nicely and by doing which work I would get happiness?" I feel inventions of new products give me happiness.
- When you're doing something for yourself, or your best friend or family, you're not going to cheese out. If you don't

love something, you're not going to go the extra mile, work the extra weekend, and challenge the status quo as much.

- Your work is going to fill a large part of your life, and the only way to be truly satisfied is to do what you believe is great work. And the only way to do great work is to love what you do. If you haven't found it yet, keep looking. Don't settle. As with all matters of the heart, you'll know when you find it. And, like any great relationship, it just gets better and better as the years roll on. So keep looking until you find it. Don't settle.

World

- I am not a political leader of 62's who might have seen the whole world but this is sure that when I was 25 years old the situation was this kind. But if I would have been then like today with more information then I would have taken a much better decision. I also know that on becoming 35 years age yet I would then think of future as today. I can keep strong belief in my conclusions. It may be that I like myself and hence do no worry of the change.
- I think it's quite a natural curiosity for adopted people to want to understand where certain traits come from. But I'm mostly an environmentalist. I think the way you are raised and your values and most of your world view come from the experiences you had as you grew up. But some things aren't accounted for that way. I think it's quite natural to have a curiosity about it.
- I think it's brought the world a lot closer together, and will continue to do that. There are downsides to everything; there are unintended consequences to everything. The most corrosive piece of technology that I've ever seen is called television-but then, again, television, at its best, is magnificent.

Woz

- I met Woz when I was 13, at a friend's garage. He was about 18. He was, like, the first person I met who knew more electronics than I did at that point. We became good friends, because we shared an interest in computers and we had a sense of humor. We pulled all kinds of pranks together.

Woz and I

- Woz and I very much liked Bob Dylan's poetry, and we spent a lot of time thinking about a lot of that stuff. This was California. You could get LSD fresh made from Stanford. You could sleep on the beach at night with your girlfriend. California has a sense of experimentation and a sense of openness—openness to new possibilities.
- Woj and I have many differences but we also have many similarities and in this way we are very close to each other. We are like the stars that come close now and then. It is not only about the computers but we also love poems of Danloyn and we discuss about it a lot. This is California and here you can get Stanford flesh L.S.D. or spend you night with your lover on a sea shore. In California, there had always been a conservativeness and at the same time an openness for new thinking. Apart from poems I also had interest in eastern mysteries whose effect would be seen at the same time. When I was studying in Oregon. Reed College, At that time Timothy Leary, Richard Alpert and many other intelligent people were the topics of discussions. We would try to find out the truth of their lives. In those times students of this country from all colleges have read books like '*Diet for a Small Planet*'.
- Woz is living his own life now. He hasn't been around Apple for about five years. But what he did will go down in history.

❑

Year

- Each year has been so robust with problems and successes and learning experiences and human experiences that a year is a lifetime at Apple. So this has been ten lifetimes.

You

- You can't just ask customers what they want and then try to give that to them. By the time you get it built, they'll want something new.
- You didn't have seconds, you had three weeks. The universe was created in a third of that time.
- You explained to the fire marshal that we're in here changing the world.
- You have to work hard to get your thinking clean to make it simple. But it's worth it in the end because once you get there, you can move mountains.
- You just are yourself, and you work with other people. If you're inspiring to other people, it makes an impression on them. For example, I hear people at Disney talking about what it was like to work with Walt. They loved him. I

know that people at Pixar are going to talk about their days with John Lasseter in the same way. Who knows? Maybe someday somebody will feel that way about working with me. I have no idea.

- You just make the best product you can, and you don't put it out until you feel it's right. But no matter what you think intellectually, your heart is beating pretty fast right before people see what you've produced.
- You know how you see a show car, and it's really cool, and then four years later you see the production car, and it sucks? And you go, "What happened? They had it! They had it in the palm of their hands! They grabbed defeat from the jaws of victory!" What happened was, the designers came up with this really great idea. Then they take it to the engineers, and the engineers go, "Nah, we can't do that. That's impossible." And so it gets a lot worse. Then they take it to the manufacturing people, and they go, "We can't build that!" And it gets a lot worse.
- You know, my main reaction to this money thing is that it's humorous, all the attention to it, because it's hardly the most insightful or valuable thing that's happened to me.
- You should never start a company with the goal of getting rich. Your goal should be making something you believe in and making a company that will last.
- You should try to give the best product and not stop until you are satisfied. But in fact when your product is launched in the market and your heart beats feel faster, that's normal, despite you being confident of it.
- You'll see more and more perfection of that—computer as servant. But the next thing is going to be computer as a guide or agent.

- You're blowing it with Fox News. The axis today is not liberal and conservative, the axis is constructive-destructive, and you've cast your lot with the destructive people. Fox has become an incredibly destructive force in our society. You can be better, and this is going to be your legacy if you're not careful.
- You're missing it. This is not a one-man show. What's reinvigorating this company is two things: One, there's a lot of really talented people in this company who listened to the world tell them they were losers for a couple of years, and some of them were on the verge of starting to believe it themselves. But they're not losers. What they didn't have was a good set of coaches, a good plan. A good senior management team. But they have that now.
- You've baked a really lovely cake, but then you've used dog shit for frosting.
- You've got to start with the customer experience and work back toward the technology—not the other way around.
- You'll see more and more perfection of that-computer as servant. But the next thing is going to be computer as a guide or agent.
- You've baked a really lovely cake, but then you've used dog shit for frosting.

Young

- When I was young, there was an amazing publication called the *Whole Earth Catalog*, which was one of the bibles of my generation. It was created by a fellow named Stewart Brand not far from here in Menlo Park, and he brought it to life with his poetic touch. This was in the late 1960s, before personal computers and desktop publishing, so it was all made with typewriters, scissors, and Polaroid cameras. It was sort of like Google in paperback form, 35 years before Google came along: it was idealistic, and overflowing with neat tools and great notions.

❑

Success Secrets of Steve Jobs

Imagine this is 2001 and you are holding a device which slides into your pocket with ease, and stores a thousand songs of your choice.

At the time when MP3 players reigned, and people were downloading songs off the internet, there came a device which let you store legally bought versions of your favourite songs and gave you a sound quality that was unmatched.

This is iPod for you, which today can store up to fourteen thousand songs. This revolutionary piece of electronic device was possible, just because Steve Jobs, the co-founder of Apple, Inc envisioned it.

Apart from music, his innovations extended to computers, movies, and phones, each of them making a mark of their own.

One of the strongest trait that helped Steve Jobs accomplish what he did with Apple, was his power of presentation, and he needed no tools for that. He presented his ideas in such a way that people listening were famously mesmerized and motivated to achieve the impossible.

Steve Jobs successfully ran three companies, Apple, Pixar and NeXT. He started Apple with his friend and inventor of the first Apple computer, Steve Wozniak in 1976. With him, he created the world's first highly successful microcomputer, Apple II.

NeXT, a computer and software company was founded in 1985, after Steve Jobs resigned from Apple. Pixar was acquired by him in 1986, when he became the majority shareholder in the company. Under his supervision, Pixar produced the first animated feature film, *Toy Story* in 1995.

When one has so many 'firsts' in their name, one's fame begins to precede them. His success has been attributed to a number of factors that were peculiar to his personality.

Keep Looking; Don't Settle

What Steve Jobs had the most was passion; passion to change the world. It is what pushed him forward in whatever he worked for. During a Commencement speech at Stanford in 2005, he spilled the magic beans of his success story that has been an inspiration for many, even today.

"I'm convinced that the only thing that kept me going was that I loved what I did. You've got to find what you love… Your work is going to fill a large part of your life, and the only way to be truly satisfied is to do what you believe is great work. And the only way to do great work is to love what you do. If you haven't found it yet, keep looking. Don't settle."

Many people work because they have to; only some have the courage to follow their dream and make it work. Steve Jobs was among those few, who dared to not settle. Such a characteristic is almost always inherent.

Prioritise and Organise

In the biography, Steve Jobs written by Walter Isaacson, the author wrote about his many conversations with Steve Jobs. In one such conversation, the Apple founder told the author about the importance of prioritisation in the following words, "Deciding what not to do is as important as deciding what to do."

In 1997, when he returned to Apple, the company was running on losses. The first thing that he did was cancel all the projects that were not important or did not serve any purpose for Apple. He cut down all advertising agencies and re-hired just one, the one that understood Apple's core values.

By the time Steve Jobs was done, Apple was concentrating all its energy into producing only four products. This gave the company some clarity and a direction. Above all, it helped Apple to focus on quality and this improved not just the profits of the company, but also the reputation.

Soon after, Apple came to be known for its brand value. They removed all competition; they no longer wanted to be better than others, because they decided to be unique.

Think Different

Apple was never a follower, Steve Jobs made sure of that. When he came back to Apple, he was more determined and clear headed than when he had founded the company. With every successful innovation, be it the iPod, iPhone, iMac, iTunes, or iPad, Apple created a market and became its leader, letting others follow their example.

"Think Different", an advertising slogan that was introduced in 1997, slowly became the identity of Apple. However, it was not just a slogan; it was a philosophy. Steve Jobs had once said, "People don't want to just buy personal computers anymore. They want to know what they can do with them, and we're going to show people exactly that."

This is how different Steve Jobs dared to think. He is said to have never relied on market analysis or focus groups. He, in fact, knew exactly what would work in a market that did not even exist in real-time yet.

Virtue in Simplicity

If one asks why Apple was so successful, the answer lies in their philosophy and core values. No matter how many complex designs went into making a product look simple, Steve Jobs wanted the use of Apple products to be an adventure for the end users.

In an interview with Business Week in 1998, he was quoted as saying, "Simple can be harder than complex: you have to work hard to get your thinking clean to make it simple. But it's worth it in the end because once you get there, you can move mountains."

After 1997, every product that Apple launched, made history. The employees felt connected to the company more than ever and were enthusiastic about whatever they worked on. The reason was Steve Jobs and his valuable aphorisms. He strongly believed that the quality of any product should never be compromised and that is what he instilled in all his employees.

Saying No to a Thousand Things

"Innovation comes from people meeting up in the hallways or calling each other at 10:30 at night with a new idea... It's ad-hoc meetings of six people called by someone who thinks he has figured out the coolest new thing ever and who wants to know what other people think of his idea. And it comes from saying no to 1,000 things to make sure we don't get on the wrong track or try to do too much. We're always thinking about new markets we could enter, but it's only by saying no that you can concentrate on the things that are really important."

These were the words of wisdom by Steve Jobs in a 2004 Business Week interview, where he emphasized on the importance of saying "No" to a thousand things before agreeing with an idea that he was truly satisfied with. His employees would have had to work hard on something for days and it would not be accepted and they would be asked to work on it again and again until they got it right. Such an attention to quality helped Apple produce unparalleled products.

Create Insanely Different Experiences

Have you ever walked into an original Apple store and marveled at the uniqueness of your experience? Doesn't it seem more customer-oriented than sales oriented?

The first Apple Store opened in May 2001, and it was a revolution in itself. The store saw more sales on its opening weekend, which most stores could not achieve in months. What Steve Jobs gave the people with his Apple Stores was an insane experience.

What worked was that these stores did not look like normal electronic retail stores that one would expect in those days. They were built in such a fashion that people could walk in and try out the products, ask questions at the store's 'Genius Bar' and get solutions instantly. This helped them buy their products once when they were satisfied with it. Many modern-day stores are now providing similar experiences, but Apple was, as always, the first one to introduce this concept.

Engage, Interest, and Entertain

There is no doubt that Steve Jobs had a remarkable presentation style. In each of his product launches, he had the knack to engage his audience with a promise to change the way they viewed his products. He was a storyteller, almost like a magician, pulling his latest product out with a sly smile, after building up to the uniqueness of it.

At a product launch in 2007, Steve Jobs began by saying the following words that led up to the introduction of Apple's first smartphone, iPhone 1. "This is the day I've been looking forward to for two and a half years. Every once in a while, a revolutionary product comes along that changes everything. Apple has been very fortunate. It's been able to introduce a few of these into the world."

After introducing the product, which he claimed to be the smartest among all smart phones, he showed the audience what an iPhone could do. The audience seemed enthralled with this new product, which they did not know could even exist. And before anyone could realize, everyone wanted an iPhone.

Put a Dent in the Universe

Steve Jobs has been quoted in his book, Steve Jobs, as saying, "We're here to put a dent in the universe. Otherwise why else even be here?" He surely lived up to his words. His revolutionary work in the field of technology is admirable. He always encouraged his employees to reach for the stars.

John Sculley, a former CEO at Apple was hired by Steve Jobs in 1983 by being asked one simple question, "Do you want to sell sugar water for the rest of your life, or do you want to come with me and change the world?" He was the president of PepsiCo at the time.

Steve Jobs had one great quality which he used very wisely. He knew how to persuade people to do what he wanted them to do.

Death Gives Perspective

"When I was 17, I read a quote that went something like: 'If you live each day as if it was your last, someday you'll most certainly be right.' It made an impression on me, and since then, for the past 33 years, I have looked in the mirror every morning and asked myself: 'If today were the last day of my life, would I want to do what I am about to do today?' And whenever the answer has been 'No' for too many days in a row, I know I need to change something." This is a part of a speech that Steve Jobs gave at Stanford in 2005.

He was diagnosed with cancer in 2003, and it changed his perspective not just toward life, but toward his work as well. He began to reassess his work choices, and decided that he would eliminate all things that do not serve his purpose or what he does not want to do. When one stops doing the things that they don't want to do, they are able to find more time for what they love. And as Steve Jobs believed, if you love what you do, chances are that you will succeed.

Connecting the Dots

Whenever one looks back at life, some things that did not make sense then, make sense in the present. We often wonder that we would never have reached where we are, had we not done things the way we did. This outlook almost always gives people a positive perspective when they look at life regretting not having done things differently.

At the Stanford Commencement Speech in 2005, Steve Jobs connected his dots and admitted how it helped him to achieve all that he did at Apple, "You can't connect the dots looking forward; you can only connect them looking backward. So you have to trust that the dots will somehow connect in your future. You have to trust in something—your gut, destiny, life, karma, whatever. This approach has never let me down, and it has made all the difference in my life."

The Future is Now

To do different, one has to think different. One has to forget everything that they have been told to do and begin doing what they really want to. Those who are able to replace the "should" or "have" from their to-do-list with "want" and "will" are able to achieve the unthinkable.

Following are the words by Steve Jobs that resonates his philosophy on life in general, “When you grow up you tend to get told that the world is the way it is and your life is just to live your life inside the world, try not to bash into the walls too much, try to have a nice family, have fun, save a little money. That’s a very limited life. Life can be much broader, once you discover one simple fact, and that is that everything around you that you call life was made up by people that were no smarter than you. And you can change it, you can influence it, you can build your own things that other people can use. Once you learn that, you’ll never be the same again.”

And he wasn’t.

❑❑❑